Mercy MacDonald sat down to wait for Hawkin's return. She saw that the captain's screen, like Betsy arap Dee's, was displaying their next port of call. It was a different view, though; probably it was what was being seen, in real time, by *Nordvik's* bow cameras.

She knew well enough what Slowyear was going to be like. Like everybody else on *Nordvik*, she had pored over its statistics for hour after hour, partly out of generalized curiosity, partly looking for a reason to make it her home for the rest of her life — or for not.

MacDonald knew that the bad thing about Slowyear was the very thing it was named after. Slowyear had a very slow year indeed. The planet was a good long way from its sun, and took a good long time to circle it — nineteen standard years, just about.

Fortunately for the hope of any life on Slowyear, its orbit was nearly circular. "Nearly" circular still wasn't quite. The small difference between elliptical and round was critical. It meant that the planet had winters, and it had summers. And when you said "winter", she thought, biting her lip, you weren't talking about three or four chilly months. You were talking *nasty* At aphelion the planet was moving slowly, like a yo-yo at the top of its climb, and Slowyear stayed at that distant point for nearly five standard years. Five bitter-cold Earth-time years of hiding underground.

Ask your bookseller for these BANTAM SPECTRA
titles you may have missed:

LIFELINE, by Kevin Anderson and Douglas Beason
THE TRINITY PARADOX, by Kevin Anderson and Douglas Beason
NIGHTFALL, by Isaac Asimov and Robert Silverberg
IRIS, by William Barton and Michael Capobianco
FELLOW TRAVELER, by William Barton and Michael Capobianco
CONSIDER PHLEBAS, by Iain Banks
USE OF WEAPONS, by Iain Banks
MARS, by Ben Bova
EARTH, by David Brin
RENDEZVOUS WITH RAMA, by Arthur C. Clarke and Gentry Lee
RAMA II, by Arthur C. Clarke and Gentry Lee
THE GARDEN OF RAMA, by Arthur C. Clarke and Gentry Lee
THE REAL STORY, by Stephen R. Donaldson
FORBIDDEN KNOWLEDGE, by Stephen R. Donaldson
WHEN GRAVITY FAILS, by George Alec Effinger
FIRE IN THE SUN, by George Alec Effinger
THE EXILE KISS, by George Alec Effinger
THE HOST, by Peter Emshwiller
IN THE WRONG HANDS, by Edward Gibson
THE DIFFERENCE ENGINE, by William Gibson and Bruce Sterling
DESOLATION ROAD, by Ian McDonald
STOPPING AT SLOWYEAR, by Frederik Pohl
THE SINGERS OF TIME, by Frederik Pohl and Jack Williamson
THE FACE OF THE WATERS, by Robert Silverberg
HYPERION, by Dan Simmons
RUSSIAN SPRING, by Norman Spinrad
RAISING THE STONES, by Sheri S. Tepper
STAR OF THE GUARDIANS, VOLUME I: THE LOST KING, by Margaret
    Weis
STAR OF THE GUARDIANS, VOLUME II: KING'S TEST, by Margaret
    Weis
ON MY WAY TO PARADISE, by Dave Wolverton
SERPENT CATCH, by Dave Wolverton
STAR WARS, VOLUME 1: HEIR TO THE EMPIRE, by Timothy Zahn
STAR WARS, VOLUME 2: DARK FORCE RISING, by Timothy Zahn

STOPPING AT SLOWYEAR

Frederik Pohl

SPECTRA™

BANTAM BOOKS
NEW YORK • TORONTO • LONDON • SYDNEY • AUCKLAND

STOPPING AT SLOWYEAR

Chapter One

The ship was called the *Nordvik* (though no one aboard it remembered why), and it was a big one. Even if you didn't count the thrusters on the outriggers astern, or the projectors for the Bussard collection cone at the bow, it was more than a hundred meters long; if just the habitable part of *Nordvik* had set down on any football field on Earth it would have lapped over at both ends. That would never happen, though. It had been a good many centuries, Earth time, since *Nordvik* had been anywhere near its home planet, and there was very little chance that it would ever return. It also wouldn't happen because *Nordvik*, or any ship like it, could never set down on any planet anyway. All those ancient starships were built in space and lived all their lives in space — mostly interstellar space, at that — and sooner or later they all died in space.

More likely it would be sooner, thought Mercy MacDonald as she slammed her door in the face of Deputy Captain Hans Horeger. What MacDonald didn't want to do was die when the ship did. She had lived aboard *Nordvik* for twenty-seven years, ship's time — never mind the time the outside universe went by; she didn't want to think about that — twenty-seven years and eight planetary systems, and it was time to find some comfortable place to settle down. With some suitable man, she hoped. But not just any man. Certainly not with the fat and lecherous — unselectively lecherous, which made it worse — Deputy Captain Hans Horeger.

The first thing MacDonald did was make sure the door was well locked behind her, with Horeger on the other side. The second thing was unwrap the towel she had clutched around her as she dashed out of the shower stall and dab at her sticky body. The bastard hadn't even let her rinse before he began grabbing. It wasn't much use. She moistened a cloth in her washstand, but you never could get all the soap off with a cloth. She resigned herself to going around sticky until her next turn at the showers.

It wasn't hard to do that. She'd had plenty of practice. The people who couldn't resign themselves to aggravation didn't last long on a tramp starship; and there were always plenty of tranks available in her medicine chest.

She swallowed one, sighed, and set to work. Naked, she sat down at her desk to begin keying up the ship's trade-goods manifest for the next planetfall. Concentration came hard. Horeger had not given up. She could hear him scratching at the door. She could even hear his voice; it was too low-pitched to carry, but that didn't matter. She knew what he was saying, and the occasional words that filtered through — "bitch" and "tease" and even that word he used as a final argument, "love" — were all words she had heard from him before.

It made her laugh. She knew just what he was doing out there. She could picture him crouched at her door, lips close to the crack, hands cupped around his mouth so that the rest of *Nordvik's* people wouldn't hear. As though any of them failed to observe his unrelenting pursuit. Especially his wife, Maureen.

Mercy MacDonald stood up and dressed quickly in fresh clothes, not because there was anyone to see but because she intended to speak to Horeger and obscurely did not want to do so naked. She looked at herself in the mirror while she was pulling on the blue coverall. Figure still good, chin clean, eyes clear — not bad for forty-five and a bit, she thought. The coverall, on the other hand, needed mending again at the shoulder seams; she would have to do a good deal of patching, she thought, to get herself ready for a planetfall. She listened at the door for a moment, then called, "Leave me alone, Hans. It's over. If you're that horny, go find Maureen."

But he didn't answer.

"Why, you bastard," MacDonald said to the door, suddenly angry when she realized he had given up. She didn't have any legitimate reason for the anger. She had certainly made it clear to him that furtive sex when his wife wasn't looking didn't satisfy her anymore, especially when she discovered she was sharing him also with her best friend...but why had he given up so easily?

* * *

One of the worst features of life aboard *Nordvik* was that among the fifty-six human beings who lived on the starship, adult males were a distinct minority. There were only twenty-two of them, against thirty-one adult women — adult enough, anyway. There were also three children (would be four in a week or two, MacDonald reminded herself, as soon as Betsy arap Dee delivered herself), but the ones already born were all girls, which would some day make the balance even worse. Would, that is, if no one else jumped ship, or if they didn't recruit any new people at their next stop; but that was for the future. Meanwhile the oldest child, at eight, was still too unripe even for Hans Horeger's attention.

Facing odds of that sort was a bad deal for the nine women without regular mates. Mercy MacDonald didn't like being one of them.

She hadn't always been. She'd had a husband for a good many years; in fact, both she and Walter were among the handful who were said to own a piece of *Nordvik's* keel. Apart from the doddering old captain there was no one else left aboard who, like Mercy MacDonald, had signed on when the ship first launched from Earth orbit. Counting the three children, eleven of the ship's complement were ship-born; all the rest had been picked up at one planetfall or another along the long, twisted way.

That was just one more injustice to swallow. Seniority should have counted for something. Even not factoring in the datum that MacDonald was probably the smartest and most able person aboard; even not adding on the intangible fact that she was also just about the most loyal person in the ship's complement, which she had proved by not jumping ship, not even at Hades, their last port of call, when twenty-three others were finally sufficiently fed up to pay off... including her own husband.

Neither brains nor loyalty had paid off for her, though. MacDonald was still no more than eighth or ninth down in the ship's hierarchy. As "purser," whatever that ancient title meant, she was head of the trading section, to be sure, but that meant nothing when the ship was between planets.

She thought for a moment about Hades. She had been tempted to leave with the others there; *Nordvik* was running poorer and less hopeful every year, and there was certainly no future aboard for anyone.

But Hades had been the wrong place. Hades didn't have much good land. Most of the planet was rocky hills and desert, and everything good had been nailed down by the first settlers. For whom everybody else worked — at low pay, when they could get any pay at all. All the promising planets were well in the past, MacDonald told herself. The longer *Nordvik* traveled, the worse the places it visited seemed to get. It was even possible that this new one they were coming up on would be even drearier than Hades.

It wasn't the first time that notion had occurred to her. She had even thought it during the wretched weeks when they were orbiting Hades, with her husband and herself snapping at each other whenever they were in earshot. She might well have paid off there herself...if Walter hadn't.

There had almost been a mutiny after Hades. A near half of the crew were urging tottering old Captain Hawkins to give up the whole idea of trading with future planets. They wanted either to settle down on one of the colonized worlds, or even to find some new one from the old robot-probe reports and start a colony of their own. That was when Hans Horeger had become the actual captain, in all but name. He was the one who stirred everyone up to go on.

Anyway, it wasn't a good idea. Nobody was settling new worlds right now. There were at least a dozen that the robot probes had identified by now, and maybe more reports still coming in from stars still farther away. But by now everybody knew how hard it was to start a colony in a world where no human being, no creature from Earth at all, had ever lived before. The rage for colonizing had worn itself out centuries (Earth-time centuries, at least) before.

Oh, no doubt the pioneering spirit would blossom back to life again — some time — some later time, maybe a few centuries down the pike, when all the new worlds were themselves beginning to bulge at the seams and the adventurers and the malcontents would yearn to move on. But not just yet. And definitely not with the discouraged, tired, aging crew of the starship *Nordvik*.

Mercy MacDonald shook herself and got back to work. Maybe Slowyear would be better.

Maybe it wouldn't, too, because tramp starships like *Nordvik* didn't get to the better worlds. Ships like *Nordvik* didn't have any real reason for being anymore. Ships like *Nordvik* were fossils. The only reason their cooperative had been able to buy it in the first place was that whole class of starships had already been made obsolete by the new grid-function vessels that could actually land on a planet's surface, at least when the planet was big enough and prosperous enough to afford a landing system. *Nordviks* were a disappearing breed, good for nothing but wandering around the poorest and least developed colony worlds, in hope of transacting a little business and replenishing their supplies so they could wander a little farther.

But as she patiently checked over the invoices, MacDonald wondered whether even a poor world would be poor enough to want to buy any of the things they had to sell. Some of the appliances and machines aboard *Nordvik* were ten or fifteen years old — ship's time — and technology had progressed beyond them wherever they had gone. Their trade goods were almost as obsolete as the ship. There were 2300 pieces of "scrimshaw" — the novelties the ship's crew made for themselves, to sell and to pass the time between stars — including poems, art objects, and knitted goods. There were eleven thousand, almost, varieties of flowers, fruits, ornamental trees, vegetables, and grasses, the most promising of them already setting new seeds in the refresher plots. There was a library of nearly 50,000 old Earth books in the datastore — assuming anybody on this new planet read books anymore; at Hades that part of the cargo had been a total loss, which was one of the reasons why MacDonald thought the planet was so well named. (But they were good books! MacDonald had read six or seven thousand of them herself, one time or another, and they'd made the long travel times endurable for her. Almost.) There were machines to sell to be copied (if ancient Earth machines had any value anymore) and, most of all, the huge store of data that covered every branch of human knowledge, from medicine to anthropology to combinatorial mathematics (also, sadly, subject to being deflatingly out of date).

If you put a cash value on all *Nordvik's* wares (as MacDonald had to do, to figure out what to trade for what) that had to be easily thirty or forty million dollars' worth of goods even after you discounted the holds packed with stuff that probably wasn't ever going to sell to anyone, anywhere.

But the value of a commodity was what it would fetch in the market, and who knew what these Slowyear people would be willing to pay?

She was glad to be interrupted by the ship's bell, less glad when it was Hans Horeger's flabbily hairy face that appeared in the corner of the screen. "Oh, shit," she said. At least it wasn't a personal call; it was one of his incessant all-ship addresses.

That didn't make it much better. She resignedly saved her worksheet and let Horeger take over the full screen. He had got dressed after their little interlude in the showers, anyway. Now he was wearing his public face, calm, self-possessed and not at all like the frantic breast-grabber whose sweaty hands had been all over her twenty minutes before.

"Shipmates," Horeger was saying, yellow teeth gleaming between mustache and beard, "I have just received another communication from our next port of call at the planet of Slowyear. We're still at long range, but reception is better now and the news from them is all good. They say they haven't had a ship call in a long time. I don't know how long, exactly, because they use their own calendar. But long. And they're thrilled we're coming. They're a good size for us, too. They've got a world population of half a million or so. That's kind of funny," he said, in that chatty, endearing style that endeared nobody, "because they've had twelve or fifteen generations to build up their numbers, but it could have been a lot worse." Of course it could have, MacDonald thought. It could have been zero. Slowyear wouldn't have been the first planet to die out between visits, leaving the next wanderer to arrive that way high and dry. "Anyway that's half a million *customers*. Good ones, friends! They're farmers. Farmers and stock raisers, and that means they won't have a hell of a lot of industry so I'm counting on selling a lot of our machine cargo there. Let's take a look at what Slowyear is like."

He waved a hand, and under his chin the planet's stats appeared: An F8 star; a planetary surface gravity very close to Earth normal; an atmosphere a little denser, but with a slightly lower partial pressure of oxygen. "See what it says about the primary?" he invited. "It's *bright*. So those worrywarts among you can rest easy — we won't have any trouble refueling there."

"Meaning worrywarts like me," Mercy MacDonald told the screen, since she had been telling Horeger for months that if they didn't refuel pretty soon their next stop would be their last.

She might have said more, because talking back to Horeger on the screen was one of the habits that had become standard for her — and a lot less maddening than talking to Horeger when he could hear — but it dawned on her that the faint tapping sound she heard was someone at her door.

For a nasty moment she feared it might be Horeger back again. Impossible, of course; there he was blithely pontificating away in real time on the screen. When she opened the door she was pleased to see that it was little Betsy arap Dee, as close as she had to a "best friend" on *Nordvik*. "Hi," she said, welcoming —

Then she got a better look at Betsy's face. "What's the matter?" MacDonald asked sharply, suddenly afraid.

Betsy was holding her swollen belly. "The baby," she sobbed. "I'm spotting, and I *hurt*. Can you help me get to the sickbay, please?"

By the time Mercy MacDonald got her friend to the room they used for a sickbay, Sam Bagehot, the closest thing they had to a nurse, had an obstetric bed ready and Danny de Bride, their approximation of a doctor, was fretfully studying the obstetric displays from their medical database.

De Bride wasn't a real doctor, but he was the best *Nordvik* had left after the mass desertion on Hades, and he had at least long since read through all the gynecological section. "I hope I know what I'm doing," he gritted to MacDonald as the nurse guided Betsy's feet into the stirrups and he played with the fetoscope earphones in his hand.

"I hope so, too," MacDonald said, but not out loud. Out loud she only whispered encouragingly in Betsy arap Dee's ear. Whether her friend heard her she could not say. Betsy's eyes were closed, her forehead was cold and clammy and she was moaning.

De Bride was muttering something to his nurse, but MacDonald missed it. Over their heads Horeger was still prattling noisily away on the screen. "What?" she demanded.

"I said she's hardly dilated at all," de Bride complained.

"And I'm not getting any fetal heartbeat," said Sam, holding the metal disk on Betsy's belly and watching the readout.

"Oh, shit," said de Bride. "What do you think, Sam? Do I have to do a C-section? I've never even seen one!"

"You'll see one now," his nurse told him. "Mercy, give me hand. You take care of the instruments while I handle the anesthesia, will you?"

The "will you" part was only politeness. There wasn't any real choice. If there had been, Mercy MacDonald would have been out of there long before the cutting started, but under the circumstances she was present for it all.

She had never seen anyone deliberately slice into the flesh of another human being before. There was less blood than she had expected, but still a great deal of blood; it went faster than she had imagined, but still a long business of de Bride muttering angrily to himself as he inexpertly pushed muscle walls and tissues out of the way and fumbled for the little scarlet gnome curled up inside Betsy's abdomen. MacDonald was both horrified and fascinated — yes, and something else, too. Almost even envious. For here was silly little Betsy arap Dee bringing a whole new person into existence. Marvelously! Wonderfully. Enviably....

For a moment MacDonald almost forgot the gore, didn't hear de Bride's steady muttering to himself or Horeger's orating from the screen. She could do this, she told herself. She could have done it years earlier, when she still had Walter to be a father; could still do it, maybe, if she didn't take too long getting it started —

"Here," said de Bride suddenly. "Hold it while I cut the cord."

MacDonald found herself with that purple-red little creature in her unpracticed hands. She blinked down at it, wondering. It wasn't until de Bride said, shamefaced, "I couldn't save it, you saw that. Maybe it twisted in the womb, you know? And the cord strangled it?" that she realized the baby she was holding was dead.

She stood frozen, until the nurse told her that she might as well put the tiny thing down. Then she did as she was told, and began to clean the bloodstains off the arms of her blue coverall (now really ruined, she thought regretfully) with a dressing. She didn't look at Betsy arap Dee, now being sewn glumly back together. She was watching Hans Horeger's face on the screen, listening as intently as if she cared about anything he might say.

"We're still about two light-weeks away," he was saying. "Call it three thousand a.u. We'll be there in eight months, just about. Friends, I feel in my bones that this is going to be the stop that pays off for all the others. They're going to be crazy about us!"

From behind Mercy MacDonald, Sam Bagehot said, "They'd better be."

Chapter Two

Actually, the people on Slowyear pretty nearly were going crazy over the approaching ship, or at least some of them were, though it would be many weeks before *Nordvik* entered orbit. Mostly it was the young ones who were working up steam on the subject, though even among them there were quite a few who had too many other things on their minds to get excited over the prospect of a visiting interstellar ship.

For instance, there was Blundy. Blundy had his mind full of other things, which not only weren't the approaching *Nordvik*, but weren't even the wife who was waiting for him in the summer city, much less the seventeen hundred things he was supposed to keep his mind on — namely the long ambling column of sheep he was herding into town for shearing and slaughter. Hans Horeger had been right about that. The people of Slowyear spent a lot of time farming their fields and tending their livestock, stocks, but where Horeger went wrong was that they didn't stop there. To the people aboard *Nordvik* a word like "shepherd" meant a beardless boy or a doddering old man with a stick, not someone riding in a computer-guided, hydrogen-fueled crawler who led his flock with a radio beacon keyed to the receivers implanted in each nose. The people of Slowyear had their high technology, all right; they just didn't show it off.

In that Blundy was like his planet, because he didn't show off all his strengths, either. Blundy was short and broad, with a body that was all muscle and almost no fat. The muscle didn't show. If you ever picked him up you would be surprised to discover how much he massed — if he allowed you to take the liberty of trying to pick him up. There wasn't much chance of that. Trying it would most likely turn out to mean that you were stretched out on the ground in front of him, gazing stupidly up as you wondered if anyone else had felt the earthquake.

What Blundy was thinking about on his home-bound trip was politics. He had plenty of time to think, of course, because what he was doing took very little of his attention. There was hardly any local traffic on the road this far from the city — a few tractor-trailers on their way to and from the fishing villages on the coast and almost nothing else — and anyway the crawler's computer did most of the driving. Blundy could have been thinking about many things because he *was* many things — not the least of them, a celebrated entertainer on the view screens. But what drew his imagination just then was his political planning.

Because he had been off with the flock for the four seventy-day months that were his taxtime he was beginning to feel eager to get back into his political incarnation again. He was trying to find a theme for a campaign. If he could work out the right subjects to talk about he would then, he calculated, do well to take the town auditorium for a speech the next night — if the auditorium was finished, as his helper, Petoyne, had told him it would be when they talked on the radio; if Petoyne had been efficient enough to reserve it for him.

There remained the difficult question, which was what the speech should be about. It had to be *important*. His followers would expect no less.

But what could he say that would sound important enough to shock them all into life?

Because his mind was far from what he was doing, he almost missed the traffic warden standing in the road before him. The man's hand was held sternly up and he was scowling.

Blundy slowed the crawler; he hadn't noticed that they had just passed the highest point in the pass. Other roads joined them there, and there was a tractor-trailer train of construction material waiting to cross before him. Blundy leaned out of the cab window to give the warden a quizzical look. Then the warden recognized him. He gave Blundy an embarrassed salute and waved him on.

Blundy waved his thanks to the warden and his apology to the other driver, who would now have a good long wait for the flock to clear the crossing. He didn't refuse the courtesy, though. It was a real nuisance to try to halt a procession of seventeen hundred sheep.

Then, as they began their descent into town, on impulse Blundy opened the cab door and jumped out to stretch his legs. The computer would be quite capable of following its programmed route without him, and he thought better on his feet.

Blundy landed easily on the packed dirt beside the stock road. He stretched and took a deep breath, letting the tractor and its trailer crawl past him at their two-kilometer-an-hour trudge. The road itself had been repaved since the last time he had come by, four months earlier, with the much shorter line of sheep heading out to the eastern pastures. Now there were beginning to be an occasional high-speed vehicle passing by in both directions — not at high speed here, though, not as they squeezed past the shambling line of sheep, careful of the occasional willful stray. There weren't many strays, Blundy saw with satisfaction. The flock was obediently following the bellwether radio in the trailer; and the dogs were properly patrolling between sheep and vehicles to keep them off the paved road and on the grassy verge.

Then Blundy pressed two fingertips to his lips. It was what he did when he got an idea.

"Like sheep," he said, half-voicing the words past his nearly closed lips. "Like sheep we stray in all directions, pointlessly and ignorantly, without a real goal, wandering until we die — "

No. It was the right sort of note to strike, but certainly not "until we die." There was too much dying going on all the time as it was. He scowled at the flock and tried again " — wandering without goal or direction. How can we find a goal worth attaining?

What can lead us as surely as the radio call leads the flock to — "

No again, *positively* no. Wrong image entirely. What the call led the sheep to was the shearers' sheds for all and the slaughterhouse for most. He was getting back to death again, and that was no good.

Still, he had the feeling that there was something there that he could use. It was just the kind of quick, elucidating metaphor that his political audiences loved: the radio beacon that guided the sheep standing for the purpose that would carry the voters with him. And there was something more there waiting to be expressed. Something about sheep going astray was tickling his mind, some phrase he had heard once that had come out of some old book...

Murra would know. "The hell with it," he said, meaning for now; he would ask Murra, out of her vast reading in the books that no one else bothered with, and then maybe it would all come clear.

He looked around, pleased at the sight, pleased to be going home again after taxtime. Looking down into the valley, he thought the broad Sometimes River had dropped a good deal since the last time he had passed this way. It was still well over its summertime banks, a hundred meters of flood rushing furiously downhill, but nothing like the raging torrents of first melt he had seen four months before. The glacier on the west wall was showing the signs of advancing warmth, too; it had retreated half a kilometer at least. He squinted at it until he thought he had found the spot under its lip where, at the end of the summer before, he had shared a cabin with the woman who had then been his new and brightest love.

That had been a long time ago.

Murra wasn't new and bright anymore, and the intervening winter's ice had planed away all trace of the cabin.

Then an eruption of yelping behind him made him turn. He took a good look at his flock and swore. The long line of sheep was breaking up into clots. Even though the dogs barked and nipped at their rumps the animals were tiring and so they were pausing to nibble at the fresh growth beneath their hooves. He touched the talk button on his lapel. "Give them a jolt to wake them up; they're clumping," he ordered Katiro, his replacement helper now drowsing in the trailer (and the boy was incompetent, too; why had Petoyne begged to go in early to take care of some undefined business and left him with this idiot?) A moment later Blundy heard a chorus of dismayed baaing from the flock as their radio collars gave them peremptory little electric shocks. Obediently they picked up their pace, but Blundy was annoyed. The radioman in the back of the tractor should have prevented that. If Petoyne had been in the trailer it wouldn't have happened. Petoyne would have kept an eye on the flock without being reminded. But Petoyne had had that private business that Blundy had decided he didn't even want to know about — and out of fondness for his chief helper Blundy had agreed.

It occurred to Blundy that his fondness for Petoyne was likely to become a liability.

He turned and walked after the trailer, trying to remember that glimmering of an idea — about sheep, wasn't it? But just as it was coming back to him he

heard his name called. "Hey, Blundy!" A tractor
pulling a flatbed loaded with protein supplement for
the nursing ewes in the field had slowed and the driver
was waving to him. "You've got a welcoming commit-
tee!" the man shouted, jerking a thumb back down the
hill toward the summer city. When Blundy craned his
neck to see past his own tractor, already half a
kilometer ahead, he saw that it was truth....

And that useful half-formed idea was irretrievably
gone.

There were fifty people waiting for Blundy as he
stepped aside and let the tractor proceed toward the
pens — people of all shapes and sizes, male and
female, oldsters of four and even five years and
children — well, semi-children, like his quite nearly
adult assistant Petoyne, who was waving violently to
catch his eye.

Blundy gave them all a sober salute. He didn't
smile at them. Blundy did not mind at all when his
partisans made a fuss over him, but he didn't like to
give the appearance of encouraging it. Petoyne was
hurrying toward him, whispering urgently. "Blundy?
I need a favor, and you're my best friend, so you're the
only one I can ask. Remember my dog that was getting
kind of old? Well, I didn't like the idea of killing him
just because he wasn't a pup anymore, so I did a kind
of dumb thing — "

Blundy shook his head. "Oh, hell, Petoyne.
Another dumb thing? Talk to me later," he said, not
wanting to hear. He turned to the waiting crowd,
marshalling his thoughts. There was a rock at the side

of the road, thrown there by Sometimes River when it had rampaged through at icebreak. Blundy climbed up it to get a better look at his welcomers. Were they political or theatrical? A little of each, he decided, and settled on political, not on the evidence, but because what he really wanted was to convert some of the people who admired him for his theatrical work into the ones who followed his political lead.

So, "Citizens," he said, improvising as he went along, "you know where I've been. I've been paying off my taxtime, and I ask myself: Why so much taxtime? What do the governors *do* with the taxtime? Is the winter city any bigger or more comfortable with all the taxtime work we put in? Are we ever going to start that other city on Deep Bay they've been talking about for years? Do they have a *plan?*"

He shook his head to indicate the answer, and there was a mutter of moderate agreement from the crowd — they didn't see quite where he was going, but they were willing to follow him far enough to find out. "Then why so much taxtime?" he demanded. "Why should an ordinary citizen have to spend a twentieth of his life working off his obligations to the state, when nothing ever changes for the better? I'm not talking about money taxes; we all pay income tax, and that's all right; no one complains about that. But to be required as well to put in long, weary hours at the state's business — and always in the best times of the year, when we could be enjoying ourselves — why, that is *slavery.*" Louder grunts of approval. Blundy was beginning to catch the rhythm of his own oratory, so he gave them the smile he had withheld. "But we can't discuss that as fully as it deserves now," he said. "Tomorrow night — " he glanced at Petoyne, who nodded. "Tomorrow night I'll be speaking at the assembly, and I hope I'll see you all there. But now — well, I haven't been home for four months. So if you'll excuse me — ?"

And he jumped nimbly off the rock, moving through them, shaking hands, kissing some of the younger women, with Petoyne tagging grimly behind. It all took time. When he was well clear of the last of them Petoyne tugged imploringly at his blouse. "Please, Blundy. I need a favor."

He didn't stop, because he didn't want any of the fans to catch up with him, but he looked down at her. She was a small woman — small girl, really; she hadn't yet finished her first full year. She was undersized for her age and that made her even shorter than Blundy, though he was no giant himself. "Well?" he asked.

She hesitated. "Remember my dog?" she said, as though she hadn't said it before. "They were going to put him down because of his age, you know. But he was a good dog, Blundy. I grew up with him. I thought if I could just switch him with one of the others — "

"Oh, God," he said, knowing what would come next.

It did. "They caught me," she said simply.

"You keep doing really dumb things," he said, shaking his head.

"I know," she admitted. "But I need a witness for my sentence. Now. I'm supposed to be in the execution hall in about half an hour. I've been waiting and waiting for you, Blundy — "

"They sentenced you already?" he asked, suddenly fearful for her.

She nodded. "They gave me another poison pill," she said. "I have to take it today."

It was, Blundy counted as he glumly accompanied his friend, the third time he had gone with Petoyne to the execution chamber. He was getting really fed up. Not just with the nasty business of poison pills itself, but with Petoyne for her dumbness, for the demands she made on him when he had more important things to keep him busy. "But I just got back," he complained to her as they walked, and, "I could be seeing Murra now instead of wasting my time on this crap," and, "Can't you just stay out of trouble for a while?"

Petoyne didn't answer, not directly anyway. She just stretched to look up at him, shivering in the wind that came down from the ice, her face woebegone, with sorrowful eyes and trembling chin. She didn't say that the law required her to have a witness for her execution date, because everybody knew that, or that they had long ago agreed that they were best friends, because she'd said that already. Instead she mentioned a fact: "You know you're getting pretty tired of Murra anyway." And she complained: "Who did it hurt if I just let Barney live a little longer?" And she mourned, a couple of times, in different ways, "But, Blundy, don't you see what this means? If I die of this business I could miss the *ship*. I've never *seen* a ship. By the time this one lands I could be *dead*."

He didn't respond. They walked in silence, Blundy nodding to people who recognized him, while the girl thought hard. Then an encouraging thought struck her. "One good thing," she said. "People will see you on the TV."

He gave her a scowl, intending to show that that wasn't the kind of publicity he sought, and even more to show that he didn't care what she said because he had one answer for all. "Quit complaining. It's your own damn fault," he told her judgmentally. Petoyne had known what the price was going to be, just as she had known all the other times she'd broken the laws — the two times she'd been caught and the dozens of times she hadn't.

All the same, Blundy knew how the kid felt. Petoyne wasn't just afraid of dying — well, of course she was *afraid* of that. Who wouldn't be? But worse than just the normal fear of dying was that nobody, not anybody, least of all an almost-one-year-old like Petoyne, wanted to be left out of that special once-in-a-lifetime excitement, both thrilling and bleak, that only happened when some wandering spaceship came along. And even "once in a lifetime" was an exaggeration. It wasn't that often; ships didn't usually happen along even once in a normal lifetime. There was hardly a soul alive on Slowyear who remembered the last time a ship had called, apart from the tiny and dwindling handful of five- and six-year-old dodderers.

You got to the summer execution chamber by a pebbled walk through a garden. Ribbonblossoms and roses were in bloom, thousands of them, already halfway up their two-meter trellises though spring was only five months old. The flowers didn't quite hide the chamber from people going by on the summer town's streets, but they at least kept it decently remote. Most people didn't look, though a child of thirty months or so stopped as they passed, leaning his bike against the gate to follow them with his fascinated eyes.

The marshal at the door nodded respectfully to Blundy as they entered the hall. Inside, generic music was playing in the waiting room for the execution chamber, the kind of low-pitched whispery strings Blundy associated with funerals and his almost-wife, Murra. (Funny, at first he had loved Murra's taste in music.) The waiting lounge smelled as flowery as the grounds outside. There was a pot of babywillows in the center of the room, honey-sweet, and minty greenflowers hung from ceiling baskets.

Blundy and Petoyne weren't the only ones waiting. There were four couples ahead of them, sitting quietly on the comfortable benches or pretending to be conversing with each other. They would have to wait, Blundy saw with resignation. The waiting was an extra burden, because Petoyne was getting nervouser and nervouser as she came closer to the deed itself, gripping tight Blundy's hand even though she was still technically short of her first birthday, and thus was only going to take from the children's jar.

They sat down in the waiting room, nodding politely to the ones ahead of them. The execution clerk wasn't at his desk, but almost as soon as they sat he came back in, looking around impatiently. Petoyne clutched Blundy's arm and took a quick breath, trying to read the man's face. There wasn't much on it to read, though, because the clerk was a hard-bitten old guy, easily five, maybe more, had seen everything and was surprised at nothing.

He did blink in recognition as he saw Blundy there, and quickly glanced at the monitor on his desk. Then he called a name and read a sentence: "Mossriker Woller Duplesset, for falsification of taxtime records, one in fifty." A man not much older than Petoyne stood up, hanging his head. The woman with him was nearly three — his mother, Blundy supposed — and she was the one who was weeping as the executioner escorted them out of the chamber. He paused in the doorway to give Blundy a friendly nod, then closed the door behind them.

There was a moment's silence, then the ones left began to talk. The old man got up from beside the woman who seemed to be a daughter. Wandering around the room, he paused and absently stroked the soft, downy pods of the babywillow. Then he looked more closely and frowned at what he saw. He got a cup from the water cooler and carefully moistened the roots of the plant. "They should take better care of their plants," he said severely, to no one in particular. Then his eyes focused on Blundy.

"You were just coming in this morning, weren't you?" he asked politely. "I thought so. Those were nice-looking herds you brought in." Blundy agreed that, for late spring herds, the sheep had fattened up nicely. Another — a middle-aged woman, there with a younger woman who could have been her daughter — what crime could she have committed to bring her here? — said, "They've started taking the shuttles out of mothballs," and then a couple of them began talking about what their parents, or their grandparents, had told them about the way it was the last time a ship came to call. What they did not talk about was why they were here.

Petoyne didn't join in the conversation, but she was obviously beginning to get her nerve back. "They're all adults," she told Blundy, looking around at the others in the room. "I guess they've really got something to worry about."

"You'll be an adult pretty soon," Blundy reminded her.

"But I'm not now," Petoyne said, managing a smile for the first time. "What I am is hungry. Are you?" And then, without waiting for an answer: "I bet you don't want any more lamb chops, anyway. Listen, Blundy. Let me tell you what I had last night. I made myself a scogger — broiled; a big one, with plenty of melted butter, the way you like it. And I've got a couple more in the freezer, if you want to come over tonight — I mean," she added, glancing at the door, "if everything, uh, if everything goes all right here." He shook his head. "Well, Murra's expecting you, I guess." She might have said more but then, much sooner than any of them expected, the clerk was back for another condemned and escort. The charge was assault this time, one in forty, and, surprisingly, the convict was the middle-aged woman.

"Looks like there's life in the old girl yet," Petoyne whispered, almost giggling.

Two other couples were coming in, but Blundy didn't get a good look at them because the old man was standing up and coming toward them. "I guess it's my turn next," he said apologetically. "I didn't recognize you before, but — you are Arakaho Blundy Spenotex, aren't you? I thought so. I just wanted to say how much

I enjoyed your show last winter, and, well, I might not get the chance to tell you later on."

"Of course," Blundy said, professionally warm. "Nice of you to say it."

The old man stood there, nodding like any fan who had made the approach and didn't really know what to say. "My wife really loved it. It was about the only thing that kept us going, the last couple of months," he said.

"Well, that's what it was supposed to do," Blundy said politely. "Do you recognize Petoyne here? She played Liv on *Winter Wife*. The younger daughter, remember?"

"Really?" The man seemed quite interested as he studied the girl up and down. "I wouldn't have known her," he marveled, "but then, I guess everybody says that, don't they? The augmentation and all. Well, I'm sorry to see you here, Petoyne, but you're still under age, aren't you? So it won't be so — oh," he said in a different voice, as the door opened, "I guess it's my turn. I hope I see you again."

And as the door closed behind him, the executioner and his witness, Petoyne said, "Hopes to see you again! I bet he does! Did you hear that? He got a one in five! For murder. Do you know what I think, Blundy? I think it was probably his wife he murdered, don't you think? Who else would an old guy like that kill? So maybe the show didn't keep him going all that long, after all."

Then there was another wait.

The wall screen was showing a musical group, which was getting on Blundy's nerves. He got up.

"Mind if I try to get some news?" he asked. No one seemed to care, though they all looked docilely at the screen when it came on. The oilwells on Harbor Island had been successfully uncapped, the pipelines to the refineries on the continent checked and reopened — but Blundy already knew that, because he'd seen the smoke on the horizon. The warmspring census, taken after the first crop of post-winter babies had had a chance to be born, showed a planetwide population of 534,907, the highest for that season in nine years. The water temperature in Sometime River was up to 3.5 C, and there was an 80% chance of rain —

And then the woman came back in. She was alone.

She looked very sober as she made a phone call to the crematorium. It only took a moment to arrange for the disposition of her father's remains.

Then, long before they were ready for it, it was their turn.

Inside the room Blundy sought out the cameras and found them, discreetly inconspicuous in corners of the room; the carrying out of sentences was a matter of public record. Few bothered to watch unless some relative was at risk, but Blundy squared his shoulders and assumed a properly grave expression.

The clerk looked directly at Petoyne and then looked down at his charge sheet. "Larasissa Petoyne Marcolli, first year, for willfully failing to destroy a surplus animal," he read. "Sentence is one in a thousand. Come on, and hurry up," he said, "because I want to get home sometime tonight."

Blundy rose with the girl. He took her arm firmly, though she didn't resist. They didn't say anything to

the newcomers they had left behind in the waiting
room, though Blundy could almost feel the resentment
the adults felt toward a mere one-in-a-thousand.

The execution room was the one for children, with
pretty pictures on the walls. The room itself was not
much bigger than a closet, no chairs, just a sort of
metal bench along one side of it and a low table
that contained the urn. "Up on the table, Petoyne," the
executioner ordered. "You've been here before." Petoyne climbed up, looking woebegone at Blundy,
uncomfortable on the cold metal. There were drains
around the edge of it to carry off the involuntary
excretions an executed criminal often could not help
but release, and there was a faint shit smell in the room
to show that some had. The executioner turned to take
a jar off its shelf, saying chattily over his shoulder, "I
was surprised to see you out there, Blundy, but of
course I knew you were just being a witness. I would
have been sorry if it had been the other way around,
because I really like your work."

"Thank you," Blundy said automatically. He was
mildly annoyed, though; *Winter Wife* was only a minor
work in his eyes. His social, political, and philosophi-
cal contributions were what he really prided himself
on, and yet it was the video plays that everyone praised
him for. Then he blinked. "I beg your pardon?" he
asked.

"I said, do your job, Blundy," the executioner
repeated, and obediently Blundy bent to check the jar
with its thousand little jellybean pills. The seals were
intact. When he said so, the execution clerk said
fretfully, "Well, then, break it open, man!"

And he then took the lid off the jar, and offered it
to Petoyne, who unhesitatingly thrust her little fist in,
pulled out a pill, popped it in her mouth, swallowed,

She looked suddenly lost and fearful for a moment.
Then she gave Blundy a broad, happy smile.

"Open your mouth," the executioner commanded,
and rummaged around inside it with his forefinger.
Then he nodded. "Sentence carried out," he said. "Try
not to come back here again, will you? Next time you'll
be grown up." And opened the back door to let them
out into the warm spring afternoon sun.

"You know, I'm getting to like the taste of those
things," bragged Petoyne, almost skipping along beside Blundy. "What do you want to do now? Have a
drink somewhere? Go check on the slaughtering? Get
something to eat? No," she said, watching his face,
"you're off to see Murra, aren't you? Why don't you
break it off with her, Blundy? She's such a pain."

He stopped and glowered down at her. "Leave
Murra out of it," he ordered. "And, listen, I'm not going
to this place with you again, Petoyne. You're going to
be a one-year-old pretty soon, and then you won't be
getting any one in a thousand shots anymore. So
straighten out if you want to live to see that ship come
in."

Chapter Three

When Mercy MacDonald came looking for Betsy arap Dee, she found her friend in the Lesser Common Room of the starship, working with her fingers on a scrimshaw sampler but her eyes on the picture of their next planet that was displayed on the wall screen.

"We're getting good pictures now," MacDonald commented, looking for a good way to start a conversation. They were only a couple of light-days out now; four or five more weeks and they would be in orbit, and then the frenzy of transshipping and dealing would start.

MacDonald stretched to reach up and trace the outlines of Slowyear's single great continent with a fingertip. It was more or less pear-shaped, with the widest part of the pear right around the planet's equator. "Where do you suppose the landing parties will touch down?" she asked. Betsy didn't answer, except possibly with the faintest of shrugs, so MacDonald answered herself: "Probably right near their city, here — " putting her finger on the place the radio signals came from. "It ought to be nice by the time we get there. They say it's their springtime."

Betsy finally found some words worth saying. "That would have been nice for the baby," she said, bending her head back over her sampler.

MacDonald bit her lip and tried another tack. "How about giving me a hand?" she suggested. "I need to check the special-interest programs in the store so we can see what we've got to sell."

Betsy glanced up at her. "Why? We already did that, Mercy."

"So I want to do it again. To make sure. It's not good if we suddenly discover something we over-looked after we've left, is it?"

Betsy sighed and put her sampler down. She gave her friend a level gaze. "I know what you're doing. You're just trying to keep me busy so I won't be depressed, aren't you? But you don't have to bother. I'm keeping myself busy, can't you see?"

"But you're still depressed," Mercy said reasona-bly.

Betsy nodded. "Of course I am. I'm still on this damn ship. Once I get off I'll perk right up, I promise."

MacDonald lifted an eyebrow. "You really think a few weeks on a planet will straighten everything out?"

"Who said anything about a few weeks? I'm staying."

MacDonald blinked at her in surprise. It wasn't really astonishing that Betsy arap Dee was thinking of jumping ship at Slowyear — almost everybody thought such thoughts, almost every time they made a plan-etfall. The unusual thing was that she was talking about it out loud. Even to her best friend. "Horeger wouldn't like to hear you say that," she offered. Horeger had devoted no less than five of his all-hands broadcasts to the reasons why no one should leave the ship on Slowyear, along with threats of what would happen if anyone tried.

Betsy laughed. It was a curiously somber sound. "Do you think I care what Hans likes anymore?" she asked. "Do you?"

When Mercy MacDonald had a problem that needed talking over, her confidant of first choice was of course Betsy arap Dee. But when Betsy herself was the problem, she had to turn to someone else. That somebody else had to be a friend. A real one.

The list of possible candidates was not long. The little universe of *Nordvik* was far too small to hold any strangers, but the bulk of them weren't friends, either. Not friends of Mercy MacDonald's, anyway. Betsy was certainly a friend, moody as she was since the loss of her baby. Another definite friend was the captain of the *Nordvik* — by which she certainly didn't mean nasty, grabby Hans Horeger but the *real* captain, Arnold Hawkins. So were the three old navigator/astrographers, Moira Glorietti, Yahouda ben Aaron, and Dicke Dettweiler. They'd all come aboard early in the voyage, like the captain and Mercy MacDonald herself; like them they'd voted against Hans Horeger's takeover. Also like the captain, they were getting a little elderly to be *close* friends anymore.

Then there was the larger number of those who used to be friends, of one degree or another, but had

voted for Horeger and so weren't friends anymore.
That included most of the engineers and the bio
people, both the medics and the ones that cared for
their biological stocks.   And then there were the
handful of those who had never been friends of Mercy
MacDonald's at all.   That wasn't a long list, though.
Most of the time there was only one person on it, that
person of course being Deputy Captain Hans Horeger.
There had never been a time when MacDonald thought
of Horeger as a friend (though, she was ashamed of
herself to admit, for a time she had been feeling low
enough to accept him as a lover).   There were quite a
few times when she wished him off the ship, if not
actually dead — because of his crude and meaningless
sexual advances; because he had unseated old Captain
Hawkins; and most of all because of what he had done
to Betsy arap Dee.

Captain Hawkins....

Yes, MacDonald decided, he was the one she
needed to talk to. The problem was to find him. He
certainly wouldn't be on the bridge; that was Horeger's
territory now. When she stopped by the little suite he
shared with his elderly wife, she was there but the
captain wasn't.   But Marjorie Hawkins, though not
fond of Mercy MacDonald (or of any other single
woman on the ship, her husband's advanced age
notwithstanding), somewhat reluctantly told her he
could be found in his workshop.

He wasn't there, either, when MacDonald pushed
open the door after a couple of minutes of fruitless
knocking. She could see, though, that he wasn't far.
Captain Hawkins's scrimshaw work was glass mosaics,
assembled with painstaking care and a fair number of

cut fingers. Pieces of the work were scattered all over the room, piles of glass chips of a hundred colors covering every flat surface in the room. For further indication that he was nearby, the wallscreen was on.

Confident that he was no farther than the nearest toilet, MacDonald sat down to wait for his return. She saw that the captain's screen, like Betsy arap Dee's, was displaying their next port of call. It was a different view, though; probably it was what was being seen, in real time, by *Nordvik's* bow cameras. Thousands of stars were visible, but there was no doubt which star was Slowyear's sun. *Nordvik* was still far away from Slowyear's star, much farther than Pluto was from its primary. All the same, Slowyear's star was by far the brightest thing in that part of the sky. She squinted to see if she could make out the planet of Slowyear itself, but didn't expect success. It was still too faint, probably lost in its sun's glare.

She knew well enough what Slowyear was going to be like. Like everybody else on *Nordvik,* she had pored over its statistics for hour after hour, partly out of generalized curiosity, partly looking for a reason to make it her home for the rest of her life — or for not.

MacDonald knew that the bad thing about Slowyear was the very thing it was named after. Slowyear had a very slow year indeed. The planet was a good long way from its sun, and took a good long time to circle it — nineteen standard years, just about.

Fortunately for the hope of any life on Slowyear, its orbit was nearly circular. "Nearly" circular still wasn't quite. The small difference between elliptical and round was critical. It meant that the planet had winters, and it had summers. And when you said "winter," she thought, biting her lip, you weren't talking about three or four chilly months. You were talking about *nasty*. At aphelion the planet was moving slowly, like a yo-yo at the top of its climb, and Slowyear stayed at that distant point for nearly five standard years. Five bitter-cold Earth-time years of hiding underground to stay away from the surface snow and cold and misery. Mercy MacDonald, who had not experienced any real winter since she was eighteen years old, remembered the data table that said a typical night-time winter low on Slowyear was minus 70 degrees Celsius and a typical daytime winter high was only about minus ten, and felt herself shivering in anticipation.

Of course, luck had been with the visitors on *Nordvik*. It wasn't winter on Slowyear now. The good part was that they would be reaching the planet in its late spring. There would be plenty of time to decide whether to stay or not before things got frigid.

When Captain Hawkins found her waiting he gave her an apologetic grin. "It's nice to see you, Mercy," he said, pleased. "Sorry I missed you, but that's what comes with being an old man." He made a face to express the annoying problems of being old and male, then changed the subject. "How do you like it?" he asked, gesturing at the nearly finished scrimshaw wall plaque on his easel. It was a mosaic picture of their starship, made of thousands of bits of glass, carefully cracked and mounted on a plastic board, and under it he had assembled bright red letters to spell out a motto: *Ad astra per aspera*.

"It'll sell," MacDonald said, giving her professional opinion. "What does it say?"

The captain dreamily traced the words with a fingertip. "It's Latin," he said with pride. "It means, To the stars through difficulties." MacDonald snickered, and he looked up at her with shrewd humor, enjoying the patness of the motto with her. Then he sighed. "Of course, I don't suppose they'll remember Latin on Slowyear. We'll have to translate for them — but that just makes it more interesting, don't you think?"

"I'm sure of it," she told him, glad to be able to say something kind to him that was also true. MacDonald liked the captain. He was old and feeble, sure, and she hadn't forgiven him for letting the reins of the ship fall into Hans Horeger's hands, but he was a nice man. If he had been just a little younger —

But he wasn't younger. He'd been in his fifties when he took command of the ship, back in Earth orbit. Now that he was well past eighty his principal activities were scrimshaw and naps.

He was already sitting before his scrimshaw, sorting through the pile of violet glass for just the right piece to make a background star. She cleared her throat. "Captain?"

He looked up with a smile of reluctant resignation. "You didn't just come here for my company, did you? I suppose something's the matter."

"With Betsy arap Dee," she specified. "I don't know if you know about her problems — "

"Of course I do," Captain Hawkins said, finding the right chip of purple and dabbing it with cement. "She's miserable. She didn't really want to have that baby, because Hans was the father and wanted to pretend he wasn't, and then it died. Now she hates everybody."

"She doesn't hate me!" MacDonald protested, then amended herself. "Not really, anyway. She hates the whole ship, I guess. She's talking about jumping on Slowyear."

"Yes," the captain nodded, carefully setting his new star in place.

"And so am I," she finished.

He looked up at her kindly. "Of course you are, Mercy. Did you want to ask for my blessing? You've got it. Betsy, too. There's no future for you here." He reached out and covered her hand with his lean, age-spotted one. "I'd do it myself," he said, "if I were a little younger. If Maureen would agree. As it is, I don't know if I'll even go down."

That startled her. Never before had the captain failed to touch the soil of a new planet. "But you have to!"

"Nonsense, Mercy. You don't need me. You can handle all the bargaining yourself, and anyway I'm going to have to stay aboard."

"You mean for the refueling," MacDonald said, trying to understand. "But Horeger can take care of that — "

"Not just the refueling. Rebuilding." He reached past her to the screen. "Look here, Mercy," he ordered as the schematics of *Nordvik* appeared to replace the starfield. The whole ship was outlined skeletally there, mostly white lines but with some components in yellow and green and a few flashing red. "Look at the air system. It's falling apart; we're going to have to rebuild it if we can — or buy one on Slowyear, if they have anything we can use. And water regeneration's almost as bad, and — well, Maureen tells me we're

almost out of fabrics for clothes and bedding; we'll
have to see what they can offer there, too. We need
a lot of stuff. You'll have to make some good deals for
us, Mercy."

"And if I can't?"

He considered for a moment, studying the engineering reports. "You will," he said. Then, wearily, he
flicked the screen off. "You have to. Otherwise we
don't go anywhere from Slowyear." He looked at her
face and smiled comfortingly. "It won't be so bad for
you down there. They eat bugs on Slowyear, did you
know that? Oh, they raise sheep and eat them, too, but
the only native land life forms they can eat are
arthropods. Although there's a lot of native fish, or
something like fish. They don't seem to have any cows
or pigs, by the way. Your frozen genetic materials
ought to be worth something…. And the place has a
lousy climate, and it's a pretty backward world, I think,
but you can make a life there, Mercy."

She looked at him, suddenly apprehensive. True,
she had been toying with the idea of jumping ship
there in her own thoughts…. But that was when she
had a choice. But if she didn't? If Slowyear was going
to be her last stop, ever? Make a life on a planet with
a year nearly twenty years long? Bitter winters, burning
summers, the only time the place would be bearable
at all when freeze was melting toward burn, or sweat
on its way down to chill. What kind of life would that
be?

Or (the question came uninvited to her mind), for
that matter, what kind of life did she have now?

Chapter Four

What Blundy knew for sure as he headed toward Murra's house was that Murra would be there waiting for him. She always was.

He had to look around and finally ask directions, though, because he not only couldn't find Murra, he couldn't even find their house.

Naturally she wasn't in the house they'd shared all the mean, long winter just past. That place hadn't even been a house at all, actually; it was a nasty, cramped three-room flat, not much worse than any other winter flat, but not much better, either. It had been in the winter city, dug into the caverns under the hill. No one would want to go back and live there again for many months now. Certainly not until summer drove them to it, maybe not until the next desolate winter came, when the babies born now would be getting close to puberty and just beginning to understand what they were in for when the cold came.

As it turned out, Murra wasn't even in the house he'd left her in (that one hardly more than a tent), because while Blundy was out with the flocks the building boom had reached its peak. Most of the constructions of the year before, that winter ice had crushed and spring floods had washed away entirely, had now been replaced. Now they had a real house, he discovered. Murra had moved their things into it while he was out with the sheep. It was smallish but spanking new, all their own; and of course Murra was waiting in it for him, because she always was.

What she was waiting for was to be kissed. He obliged her, wondering why a kiss seemed so much like a political statement, but she had no such reservations. She pressed herself against him as they kissed, confident she was welcomed.

In a certain sense she was; Blundy could feel his body confirming it. Whatever Blundy thought about his wife, his body found her powerfully attractive. Murra was a handsome woman: tall, ten centimeters taller than Blundy himself. She was big-boned and not exactly pretty, but very close to beautiful. Murra had a kind of Oriental cast to her face, with short, black hair and blue eyes, and when she moved it was with studied grace.

More than any of that, she was Blundy's. She proclaimed it in everything she did. She was totally supportive of him in everything he chose to do, and let that fact be known to everyone. She had a soft, cultivated, well-articulated voice; for Blundy it was her best feature, and the one that made her the exact right choice to appear in his vid productions.

All in all, she was ideal for him. He accepted that fact. It was an annoyance that he didn't always enjoy it.

When they had finished their kiss she didn't release him but comfortably whispered the latest bits of news against his lips to bring him up to date. "They're starting up the shuttles," she told him. "Ten-month infant mortality figures are up a little — around eleven point three percent — but that's still in the normal range. I hope you like your new house; I only finished moving things in last week. And, oh, yes, the Fezguth-Mokorris have broken up, he's taken up with some two-year-old and Miwa simply can't stand it."

She sounded proud. Blundy recognized the tone, because he knew what the pride came from. Both Kilowar Miwa Fezguth and Murra were among the few who could call themselves successful winter wives, the envied kind who had managed to keep their marriages going all through the cramped, everybody-in-everybody's pocket months and months of the interminable winter. But Murra's pride was double now, because, of the two of them, it now transpired that only Murra had managed to stay married through the spring. "I feel so sorry for her," she added generously, smug in her own security. "They say if you can make it as a winter wife you can make it forever, but I guess they showed that isn't true for everybody. Just the lucky ones like us," she finished with pride.

"Yes," he said, separating himself from her at last.

She gazed at him fondly. "And do you like what I've done with your new house?"

"Of course. Are they all in working condition?" Blundy asked, and she looked puzzled until she realized he meant the shuttles.

"Oh, I think so. They've been kept in a good, sheltered valley ever since the last ship came. Of course, the ice covered them every year, but the roof held." She smiled at him affectionately. "Don't worry, they'll be ready to go by the time the ship gets here. And it'll be warmspring by then — a good time to come here, don't you think? Are you going to write something about it?"

Since Blundy was used to his wife's uncanny ability to read his mind — though he was certain he'd never said anything to her about his plans — he didn't blink at that. "I've been thinking about it, yes."

"I thought you might. Of course, you know best, dear, but isn't that sort of a depressing subject?"

"Tragic," he corrected her. "That's where real drama is, after all, and I'm tired of writing all this light stuff to keep people quiet during the winter."

"I see. So you'll want to go up to the ship right away, won't you? Don't deny it, dear; who knows you as well as I do? And of course you should."

He didn't deny it. He'd already decided to put his application in, and with his standing in the community there was every chance the governor's council would approve it. He had even told Murra when he'd done it. What he hadn't told her was who he proposed to take with him on that first mission to the starship, and so he was surprised when, without a break, she went on:

"And how was Petoyne?"

Blundy misunderstood her on purpose. "She's fine. She got away with it again."

"No, of course she got away with it," Murra said, tolerant and sweet, and not in the least interested with the fact that once more Petoyne had escaped with her life, "or you would have said something right away. That's not what I mean. I mean how was she in bed?"

He glared at her. "For God's sake, Murra, she isn't even one yet!"

"I know," Murra agreed, her tone interested and a little amused. "Isn't it funny how men always like the very young ones? Is it because they're so skinny? Or so ignorant and unexperienced? Please don't be embarrassed to talk about it with me, Blundy. I've never been jealous, have I? And you know we always tell each other things like that." She smiled. "In pillow talk," she added, "because, do you realize, you haven't even looked at your new house yet? Not even at the new bed I just put in." And he knew what to do then, and wondered when it had begun to be a chore.

There were times while they were making love when Blundy's body managed to make Blundy's mind forget the fact that Murra was really a royal pain in the ass. At those times he pretty much forgot to think about anything at all, because Murra in bed was not at all like the Murra who let herself be viewed as she sat, perfumed, enrobed and regal, in her reception room. In sexual intercourse she was wild. She screamed and scratched, and she writhed and squeezed; she was everything any man dreamed of in the arts of intercourse. None of it was inadvertent, either. That had been the most disillusioning of Blundy's slow discoveries about the woman he had married. It was all rehearsed. Murra made love by script, her skills quickly and thoroughly learned. "A lady in the drawing room, a harlot in bed," she said of herself, in that pillow talk that meant so much to her, and she had herself perfectly right.

But then, when they had sufficiently worn each other out, she naturally had to spoil it all by talking.

"I wrote you a poem, my love," she told him, serene again if sweaty. "Would you like to hear it?"

"Of course," he of course said, but hardly listened as she pulled her notebook out of the nightstand and sat naked and cross-legged at the foot of the bed, reading. The poem was a typically long one. It had to do with ancient shepherds and the loving lasses they had left behind them, and it was full of graceful little turns of phrase and unexpected rhymes, but he didn't really listen. He was studying her. He observed, as though for the first time, that his wife had a wide-browed face that tapered to the chin, with large, pale blue eyes and the kind of bobbed hair that is usually seen in pictures of medieval squires. She smiled a lot as she read — faintly, enigmatically, frequently. It occurred to Blundy that Murra's smiles didn't seem to be related to anything she found humorous, only to an inner confidence that whatever happened next was bound to be nice.

She didn't ask him if he liked the poem when she was done, she only sat there, regarding him with that smiling self-confidence. So naturally he said, "It's a fine poem, Murra. Your poems are always fine."

She nodded graciously. "Thank you, Blundy, but what about you? Did you write anything while you were away?" That was the naked question he had known she would ask, so much an offense to hear. He shook his head. "Not even a political manifesto?" He shook his head again, resentfully now. Murra didn't let that put her off. She laughed, the silvery, loving, forgiving laugh that he had heard so often. "Oh, Blundy, what am I going to do with you? You don't write anything but puppet shows all winter because you need to be alone in order to do anything *serious*. Then you don't write anything at all when you're out in the boonies with all the room in the world because — Well, I don't know what the because is there, do I? Maybe then you're not alone enough out there, are you, with that pretty little Petoyne there to distract you?"

"Good night," he said, and rolled over, and pretended to be asleep.

Murra was not deceived. She snuggled down next to him, rubbing the small of his back in the way that he liked, or had once told her he liked. She was thinking. Part of her thoughts were about the fact that he hadn't really said anything *specifically* admiring about her poem, but what she was mostly thinking about was Petoyne.

Murra would not have described her feelings about Petoyne as jealousy. Murra never felt jealousy; she was far above that. She would have said that she was simply surprised. What surprised her was that Blundy hadn't become tired of the girl by now. After all, he'd seen a lot of little Petoyne all through the filming of *Winter Wife*, twenty long months from Freeze to New Year's, a show every week for two hundred weeks. Petoyne hadn't even reached puberty when they started taping; that had been the subject of one whole set of shows.

Of course, there hadn't been anything sexual between Petoyne and Blundy then. That had happened later. Blundy had not confided a date to her, but, Murra conjectured, it had probably been about the time the month of New Year's changed to Firstmelt, and with the first touch of coldspring the world began to look interesting again.

"Blundy?" she said softly, sweetly, inquiringly. He didn't answer, but she knew he was awake. "Blundy, what I don't understand is why she went out with you. A young girl like that, she should be doing her taxtime in town. What does she do about her schooling?"

"She studies in the camp," Blundy said, without turning over.

"Yes, but she can get in trouble there, can't she? I mean, this thing with the dog. It wasn't *her* dog. It was just a sheepdog, and it was too old to be any good anymore. Why didn't she let them put the silly thing to sleep, the way they were supposed to?"

He was silent for a moment. Then he said, "I guess when Petoyne loves something she hates to let go of it."

"I see," Murra said. "Yes, I see that." And a moment later she heard Blundy's regular breathing turn into a gentle snore as he really did go to sleep; but she lay awake for some time, thinking about that.

Although Murra was careful to preserve her public image of perfect, unstriving self-control, she was not at all an idle person. On the contrary. Murra acted with great and speedy force when force was needed. She simply used her force in the most economical fashion, by pushing where whatever force opposed her was weakest.

In the present case, she was quite confident that that weakest point was young Petoyne herself, and so Murra made it her business to be at the sheep pens the next day, knowing that Petoyne would be working off another stretch of her taxtime there.

The sheep pens were not the sort of place Murra generally cared to visit. The place sounded and smelled and looked like what it was, a killing field, and when Murra arrived the processing of the flock for shearing and slaughter was already well under way. These particular herds were all meat animals, smaller and more active than the larger breeds kept for milk, and so their life expectancy was always short. They were milling restlessly in the pens as they waited their turns to be shorn before being slaughtered. Murra could hear the terrified bleating of the sheep as they filed into the shearing shed and, one by one, were each rudely caught and cropped by the shearers. Their wool flopped in great flat tangled mats to the floor, sometimes reddened with blood when the shearer's giant scissors cut too close to the skin. Nude and yammering, the sheep then ran to the nearest exit, where they were sorted out — young ewes herded away to be preserved for the next lambing, the old ones and the young males on to the slaughterhouse itself.

That was where the bleating stopped forever. What remained of each animal was swiftly dealt with by men and women in bloody coveralls as the carcass was gutted, sectioned, cleaned, wrapped and sent on its way to the freezers against the next winter's needs. It was all very quick: forty-five minutes, tops, from the first touch of the shears to the ice. The speed made it merciful, Murra thought, but it did not make it any less ugly to watch.

She looked around for Petoyne, and found the girl in the wool sheds, with a dozen others lugging the mats of raw wool to a flatbed trailer.

Petoyne looked up, sweaty and disgruntled, when Murra called her name. "Oh," she said. "It's you."

"You seem to be busy right now," Murra smiled.

"Oh, is that the way it looks to you?" Petoyne nodded agreeably. "It looks that way to me, too. I'm supposed to be working now."

Murra saw with satisfaction that the girl was trying to deal with her on her own terms. She had never doubted that her will would prevail over this presumptuous child, but now it was certain. "It's really fine of you to be so sensible about it," she said. "What I don't see is why you can't be so sensible about other things."

"What particular things?" Petoyne challenged.

"Why, your *recklessness*, of course. You really should stop getting in trouble. You're going to be one soon, aren't you?"

"Next month. The eleventh of Green."

"And then you won't be taking from the baby jar anymore, will you?"

"Yes, everybody says that," Petoyne agreed. "Is that what you came here to tell me?"

"Not exactly, no. I did want to talk about responsibility, though. Our responsibility to the world we live in. I'm sure you know how important Blundy's plays are to the whole world — Blundy's and mine, really. They aren't just entertainments, you know. People rely on us. We help them keep their lives under control."

She tried to decipher the girl's bland expression, then nodded. "I know what you're thinking, Petoyne. You think I'm not really that important to the plays, don't you? You're thinking that Blundy's the one who counts and, after all, I'll be nearly four next winter, and maybe a little elderly to still be playing in Blundy's stories?" She nodded again, a friendly, understanding nod. "Yes, that's what you're thinking, all right. But the important thing here is what Blundy thinks, don't you agree?"

Petoyne shrugged. Murra allowed her one of those silvery laughs. "Oh, don't mind what I say, child," she said good-naturedly. "I have this terrible habit of reading other people's thoughts. Confess, I knew just what was on your mind."

Petoyne turned to face her squarely. "What I was thinking was that I have to finish here, so I can go home and get cleaned up and hear Blundy in the stadium tonight. Aren't you going?"

In surprise, "But, my dear, I can't go to the stadium. I have to work. But I'll hear all about it from Blundy himself. When he comes home. Because he *always* comes home, you know."

It was true that Murra had to work out her labor tax. No one avoided that, because the community always had jobs that had to be done. What was also true was that being Murra — being *Blundy's* Murra — she had almost the same privileges of picking and choosing as

Blundy himself. She used her privileges a lot more freely than Blundy did, too. Of course, she wasn't in politics, as he was, and so she could afford to be less concerned about seeming diligent.

These were the seasons of the long year when you needed privileges, too, if you wanted to avoid some such ghastly assignment as Petoyne's, because there was a lot of hard and unpleasant work to be done after the winter. Construction, for instance. Everything that the kilometers-thick glaciers had planed into rubble had to be built over again; that was hard, physical work of the exact kind that Murra would never let herself be trapped into. The farms had to be plowed and seeded — just as laboriously; the fishing fleets had to be repaired, or more often replaced with new construction — even more laborious; the roads graded, the power lines restrung, even the sewers cleared and patched. In that sort of taxtime work people sweat a lot, and that did not suit Murra.

During the harshest, earliest month of Slowyear's long vernal seasons she had made sure to get work in the hospital. At least you were always indoors there, besides which the work was not intellectually demanding and most of the time was even fairly easy. On the other hand, much of it was, by Murra's standards, rather ignoble — she loathed the bedpans, and had been repelled by her first few weeks, when she had found herself committed to the obstetrical wards. Transfer to caring for the newborns was a slight improvement, though it involved crying babies and messy diapers. Then she had worked her way up to the large wards where the dying infants were kept. At

least those brats were either comatose or heavily
sedated, which came to the same thing, but overseeing
a couple of hundred small kids in the process of dying
was simply too depressing for Murra to put up with.

Then she got the job she wanted. A position came
open in the utilities section. It was Murra's kind of
work — checking employment records for the people
who did the physical work of keeping the solar-power
plants running at maximum efficiency. She stayed
away from the actual physical labor, of course. That
kind of work was at least dirty, since you couldn't stay
neat when you were digging down to a leaking pipe
in the underground clay beds that stored the summer's
heat to feed back to the city all winter long. Some of
it was actively dangerous — maintaining the high-
pressure storage tanks where the hydrogen fuel was
kept after being electrolyzed out of glacier meltwater
by the solar energy; there weren't many accidents with
the hydrogen, but when there was one people generally died. And all of it was hard — or at least, all of it
but Murra's own part, which was spent in the air-
conditioned accounting office, with a pot of tea always
beside her, safely away from the nastiness of the actual
digging and repairing.

She even had a little vid screen of her own on her
desk, and when Blundy gave his speech she naturally
stopped work to watch. No one objected. Everyone
she worked with knew very well how important she
was to Blundy. Now and then some of her colleagues
would even take time from their own work to drift to
her desk and look over her shoulder at the screen.
They were careful not to disturb her concentration, of

course. If they spoke to her at all, it was only to say things like, "He's in good form tonight," or, "Blundy really ought to be on the council." She didn't even really hear such remarks. They were completely expected, and she acknowledged them only with an automatic nod or smile.

The burden of the speech, she heard, was a challenge to the council to make better plans for the future.

It was a pity that he hadn't discussed it with her ahead of time, she thought regretfully; it wasn't a very forceful issue. Still, he made it sound serious enough as he demanded that the pipes be laid farther underground, so that they might not freeze in the next cold, to find safer places for the fishing fleet — "to think *ahead,*" he cried, "so we don't have to start from scratch every spring, so we can make things *better* each year instead of working as hard as we can just to stay even!"

Unfortunately, the audience seemed to share her opinions of themes. Oh, they cheered him, all right, and he'd been given a really satisfactory turnout — the cameras showed that there had to be at least a couple of thousand people in the audience, with no doubt twenty or thirty times as many watching at home on their screens. But the same cameras showed that they weren't all staying. All through his talk a few were getting up and leaving. Not many. Just a handful, now and then, and they were quite polite and quiet about it...but he was losing them.

And if the cameras saw that, Blundy would be seeing it too.

Murra sighed and resigned herself. He would not
be in a good mood when he got home. So her primary
job then would have to be reassurance. She would be
supportive and complimentary rather than critical.
The little notes she had made to pass on to him — his
distracting little habit of scratching his nose every few
minutes, her suggestion that he look directly into the
camera more often, to allow for close-ups — they
would have to wait for another time.

All those burdens were easily borne. They were
exactly the things that made her indispensable to
Blundy. What was harder to bear was that, when the
speech was over, not a single one of her office
colleagues came over to congratulate her. It almost
seemed as though they had been disappointed.

Blundy himself was, though. That was apparent
from the fact that he wasn't home when Murra got
there. When he did show up, hours late, he shook his
head at the dinner she had rushed to prepare for him.
She smiled to show she didn't mind. "I suppose you've
been ruining your digestion with hawkerfood," she
said, her tone gently humorous to show that it wasn't
meant as a reproach, although it was.

He shrugged. "I was discussing the meeting with
some people, it got late, I was hungry. Murra? Do you
think I ought to hold off on any more meetings for a
while?"

"Oh, no, my dear! Look at the way they applauded
you!"

"But there wasn't a single question about anything
I said!" he complained, flinging himself onto a chair.

"All they wanted to talk about was the ship — how I thought we should receive the people, how much we should tell them, what I thought we'd gain from their visit."

She knelt beside him and said apologetically, "I'm afraid I didn't hear any of the discussion period. They cut away right after your speech."

"I wish I had!" He was silent for a moment. Then his hand reached out absently to stroke her head. "Well, what about it? Shouldn't I give it up until this ship thing has come and gone? Some of my friends think so."

Murra, who was quite sure which of his "friends" the advice was coming from, said only, "I think that must be your decision to make, my dear. Would you like to come to bed?"

He shook his head. She got up and kissed him good night, not failing to notice the faint echo of her own perfume on him.

That wasn't unexpected. Murra didn't comment. It was a fact, though, that although she had no intention of quarreling over Petoyne's attempts to replace her in Blundy's bed, she came very close to complaint when she discovered the girl had switched to wearing her own perfume.

This part of spring was a joyous time. Murra did her best to make it joyous for Blundy. As the days went on, though, it began to trouble her to observe how little time he chose to spend with her. He was always busy. Yes, she understood, Blundy needed to get away by himself from time to time — that was why she had not objected, or at least had not objected much, when he signed up to escort the flocks of pregnant ewes off to the grazing lands. (But how incongruous that Arakaho Blundy Spenotex should be a *shepherd!*) But that was then. This was now. She did her best to understand what it was that kept him away from her so much of the time (doing such strange and inferior things as helping inseminate the ewes and sod the bare lawns of the new houses — *anybody* could do them!).

It was not, of course, simply that she longed for his company. She wasn't sure she did long for it very much, really. The certainty that he would always return to her was almost as good as his physical presence, and a lot less trouble. No, what Murra jealously wanted was the privilege of making sure that Blundy's needs were met.

When she realized that what he needed most was simple-minded recreation, nothing that made demands on him, nothing that required thought, her task became simple.

She would arrange a dinner party.

Yes, a dinner party would please him. Her dinner parties always had. As soon as she had thought of it she wondered why she hadn't thought of it before, and immediately began to plan.

The guest list was the most important part, of course. No more than six people: Blundy mustn't be tired by the company. For the same reason, nobody *serious*. The party was to relax Blundy and give him pleasure, not to be *work*. The first couple she chose were Delyle and Kondi, a natural selection because they had appeared as young marrieds in *Winter Wife*.

Although they hadn't actually been married then, they'd got along with each other so well that now they were. More important, they'd got along with Blundy, too. And he liked Vennit and Ginga, too, who had the additional advantage that Ginga — Macklin Ginga Spenotex — was some sort of distant relative of Blundy's. Besides, they both were outspokenly loyal to Blundy's political ideals, though Murra doubted either of them knew just what they were. Finally she decided on her sister and her husband, though only if they were willing to leave the kids at home; she didn't want Blundy to have to share his guests' attention with children.

When she had finished her list she regarded it with satisfaction. All the guests she chose were young, attractive, and as close as possible to brainless; and the list did not, of course, include Petoyne.

On the day of the party she sent Blundy about his business, without asking what that business was, and set off on an exhaustive study of the marketplace. The salad had to be the crispest, the yams the sweetest, the butter for her sauces the richest. She circled the stalls critically, looking for inspiration. She had already decided that the main dish would not be scoggers, because she had served them to Blundy too many times already in the recent past. Nor would it be anything that came from sheep, of which he had had plenty while out with the herd. She settled finally on a handsome, meter-long "fish" — they called it a salmon, though it did not resemble anything on Earth — which she steamed to a golden yellow, chilled and, that night, served with a rich sauce on a bed of greens, and was satisfied.

Almost satisfied. The food was first-rate, the guests were obligingly cheerful; and Blundy sat through it patiently. He praised the food, and carried on polite talk with the guests. But he was bored.

When Murra found out what Blundy was doing with his time she was mildly vexed.

He wasn't secretly writing, as she had hoped. He wasn't even meeting with his political allies, or even with Petoyne — not often, anyway. What the man was doing was taking flying lessons. Every day he was climbing the hill to the plateau people called the "spaceport," where the shabby old shuttles were being checked and de-mothballed, and spending hour after hour sitting at the simulator controls, with an instruction program running on his screen.

When she laughed at him he didn't get angry, only patient. "But how can you learn to operate a spaceship out of a training program?"

"How else? There's nobody alive to teach me."

"But, my dear, why should it be you to take such a risk?"

He thought it over carefully before he found the right answer. "Because I want to," he said.

As the month of Thunder warmed into the month of Green, Murra tried again and again to recapture his attention, or at least to entertain him. She didn't nag her husband; that wasn't her style. Murra's style was to be forgiving, loving, and *never* irritating — in fact, a perfect winter wife, even through coldspring and warmspring and right on through the years. She kept inventing pleasures for him — unfortunately, pleasures that he didn't seem to want.

That didn't keep Murra from going on with her project of devising entertainments for him. Some represented real sacrifices on her own part, as when she persuaded Blundy to a weekend's rafting on Sometimes River, slowly dwindling down from its coldspring flooded size. That wasn't a success for either of them. Murra managed to contain, or at least disguise, her own distaste for anything out of doors, but Blundy was not entertained. He did some mood-disguising of his own. He dutifully paddled the raft with her, shouting as loud as she when they were drenched in the rapids, smiled a lot, exclaimed appropriately at the pretty warmspring flowers that were beginning to carpet the canyonsides — and was bored again.

The sort of thing that would really give Blundy the pleasure and stimulation he needed had to be a mixture, she decided. Fun people to talk to (but not the sort of dolts she had invited to dinner), an interesting place to visit (but nothing that required too much exertion) — of course! She had it: a picnic up on the glaciers, perhaps at a place near where the shuttles were just now emerging from their winter shroud of ice.

Again she chose her guest list with the greatest care. Her first pick was Vorian, who was old but still spry, and was always willing to play chess with Blundy; besides, Vorian wouldn't be with them much longer, she was pretty sure. Then Morney, who was still pretty in spite of the fact that she was nearly three; Blundy liked being around pretty women. Importantly, she was also quite securely married to Megrith, the family doctor, who was an asset to the picnic in his own way: he loved to cook outdoors. Finally, there were Vincor and Verla, Vincor because Blundy liked him and Verla because she was Murra's sister. And this time they would be invited to bring their children. You couldn't have children at a dinner party, but how could you have a picnic without them? They were good enough children, as children went; they were winter-born kids, old enough to be reasonably civilized. (And sister Verla, though a cheerful soul and always good company, was conspicuously plain.)

Of course, when Blundy was told about the picnic he got that cold and obstinate look of his. But then he always did. And he gave in in the end.

When Blundy found Petoyne to make his apologies she was working in the insemination pens. "I'm sorry, Petoyne," Blundy told her, watching while she worked. "You know I wanted to spend your birthday with you, but I really can't get out of this picnic. Maybe I can fix it so you could come along?"

She finished with the bleating ewe, spraddled on its back with all four of its legs tied in the air, and looked up at him. "Fat chance of that," she said dispassionately. "Even if Murra would let me come I'd spoil the whole day for her. Not that I'd mind that so much. But she'd make it miserable for me, too. No," she said, "I'll spend my first birthday by myself. It's all right. I'll have others."

She filled the syringe again with the mixture of sheep semen and distilled water and moved to the next writhing ewe. Blundy knotted his brows. "Why did you volunteer for insemination? You don't have to do all this kind of scut work," he protested.

"I have to pay my taxtime off, don't I?"

"Well, sure." They all had that problem — Petoyne, Murra, Blundy, himself, everyone connected with *Winter Wife;* the show had been a great financial success, and their taxes were high. "But not this way, Petoyne. I'll be going out with the herd again, after the ship lands. You could come with me again."

"Oh," she said, "I want to get it out of the way. I think I'm going to want to stay in town when the ship's here. You know. Just to see what they have to sell; and mostly, I guess, just to see the strangers."

"That's not my idea of fun," Blundy said.

"Well, it'll be interesting, anyway. You don't get the chance to see that every day." She finished with that ewe and moved to the next; it was almost the last. "Do you know what these people from the ship are like?" she asked.

"As much as you do, I guess. No more. They're just traders, people in an old ship, trying to make a living going from planet to planet." He thought for a moment, then added, "They'll probably seem pretty strange. They're *old,* you know. I don't mean physically — I mean the time dilation — they travel pretty close to the speed of light between stars, so time slows down for them. I'd bet that some of them were already born when the first colonists landed here."

She nodded. It wasn't anything she didn't know for herself, but it needed repetition to make her believe that any living person could have been alive that long, long time ago, more than twenty-five of Slowyear's very slow years. She sighed. "Poor people," she said, finishing the last of the ewes. She patted the creature's head, then sealed the bottle of semen for return to the freezer and sat down to wait until it was time to release the dozen bleating animals. "You'd think it would be more fun for them to do it the other way," she said absently, watching them struggle against their bonds. "With a ram, I mean."

"Then we couldn't control the breeding. We get better lambs with artificial insemination," he pointed out.

She nodded, then suddenly giggled. "You could do it this way with Murra," she said, grinning up at him. "Then you could get a baby, and you wouldn't have to touch her."

Blundy cleared his throat uncomfortably. He hated it when Petoyne talked that way about Murra, almost as much as he hated it when Murra talked about Petoyne. All he said was, "What makes you think I want a baby?"

"Well, everybody does, don't they?" she said reasonably. "I do. I'll take my chances, some day. Maybe pretty soon, too," she added, "because that's the best time to do it, when you're one."

It was another allusion to her birthday, Blundy thought, the birthday that he would not be spending with her. The trouble was, birthdays were *important*. You didn't have more than four or five of them in your life, and every one marked a real change. The first long year was for growing up. The second was when you finished your education and began to get your career and your family and your life together. In your third and fourth years you were as successful and able as you were ever going to be, because the fourth birthday was retirement time — if you lived to see it — and then you just went downhill until you died.

"I've got to get cleaned up and out of here," Petoyne said. "And I guess you've got to get back to Murra."

"Well, I promised — "

"Sure," the girl said. "So long, Blundy. Have a nice picnic."

And she put her face up to be kissed, just as though nothing had changed.

He gave it up. He kissed her. "Happy birthday tomorrow," he said, turning to leave. He was a dozen paces away when he heard her call his name.

He turned to look at her. "Blundy?" she said. "I wanted to tell you — Well, if you did want to have a baby — Well, I'd be willing to have it for you."

Blundy resisted going on the picnic again at the last minute, suddenly determined to spend Petoyne's coming-of-age birthday with her after all. But it didn't take Murra long to reason him out of disappointing the others, and at last he let Murra drag him along to the hills.

And when they got out of the borrowed cat-car in a pleasant glade he seemed resigned to going along with the picnic spirit. More than that, Murra thought; he seemed quite relaxed. Even happy. He sat on a blanket under the biggest tree they could find — no more that two meters tall, because of course it had only had coldspring to grow — and gazed out over the

scene before them. Far below the Sometimes River
had at last returned to within its banks. The floodplain
all around was already planted, and the first crops well
along — good crops they would be, too, because all
that land was refreshed every year from the spring
flooding, just as ancient Egypt had been before the
building of the Aswan Dam. (Though neither Murra
nor Blundy had any clear knowledge of the country of
Egypt, much less of Aswan.)

The thing was that when at last he stirred himself
he fled from the grown-ups Murra had selected with
such care and romped up onto the glacier with the
children. Murra gazed indulgently up at them, sliding
around on the ice as they chased a little flock of pollies.
"He's so good with children," she told Verla proudly —
thoughtlessly, because then her sister had no more
sense than to say:

"I've always thought Blundy would love having
some of his own."

"Oh, certainly he would," Murra said, her lips
smiling but her eyes suddenly cold. "But we can't have
everything we want, can we? You know how it is with
Blundy and me. Can you imagine us with *children?*
We do love them so, naturally we do, but you see that
for us it would be quite impossible."

Verla nodded, seeing — seeing mostly what Murra
hadn't said. She understood, out of her own experience, why any woman would hesitate to have a baby
on Slowyear. They were unbearable in winter, when
everyone was huddled together underground, and not
much better in the hot summer, when most people
were back in the buried city again. And even if you

arranged to have the childbirth at the best possible time — right after New Year's, say, when people were getting ready to emerge into the sunlight again, as she had with her younger child — there was the high risk of heartbreak, with infant mortality on Slowyear so frighteningly high. Verla had seen a dozen of her friends go through all the mess and misery of bearing a child, and watch it like a hawk for ten long months, knowing there were three chances in ten that it would sicken and die, swiftly and inevitably, before it could walk. She'd been lucky with her own...so far.

But others had not. Two of her own friends had lost babies just in the past five months since New Year's, one of them twice.

Verla didn't say any of that to her sister. She turned to peer down into the crevasse, where the pumps were sucking the meltwater from around the hydrogen fuel complex. That would serve the shuttles, all three of them gleaming like beached whales on the flat plateau off to the west. She said, to the group at large, "It looks like everything will be ready in time for the ship."

"In time for the ship, in time for the ship," Megrith said, looking up from the fire he was starting in the grill. "That's all you hear these days, what's going to happen when the ship comes."

Old Vorian agreed. "But it's exciting, Megrith," he said. "You can't blame people. It's a good thing the ship's coming in warmspring, too. There'll be plenty of time for the unloading before the worst of the summer."

Megrith nodded. "The last one was bad, they say. You know, the one that came in, oh, eight years ago, was it? It came in winter and they had a terrible time getting the shuttles ready to fly."

"Before my time," Vorian cackled. At four and a bit, it pleased him to talk about things before his time. He craned his neck. "Isn't Blundy ever coming down?" he complained. "I brought the chessboard."

"Oh, leave him alone, Vorian," Verla said good-naturedly. "Can't you see he's having fun? Let him wear himself out with the kids — maybe he'll wear them out, too, and then we can have a civilized lunch and talk."

Her husband looked at her and cleared his throat. "Actually," he said, "I've been wanting to talk to Blundy about something — and to you too, Murra."

"Oh?" said Murra.

"I've just been wondering," Vincor said apologetically. "I mean, *Winter Wife* was such a great success — "

"They're going to rerun it, aren't they?" Verla asked.

"Yes, so they say," Murra agreed, looking at her brother-in-law. She was well aware that Vincor had always been a little envious of Blundy's success — and hers, of course; the man wanted to be a director himself. Warily she asked, "What about it, Vincor?"

"Well, I had an idea. With a huge success like that, you might as well follow up on it. You know, in a few months it'll be summer...."

"Personally," his wife put in, "I think summer's as hard to get through as winter, though it's shorter, of course."

"So what would you think of a new one for the summer? I thought of a natural title. It tells the whole story: You could call the new series *Summer Wife*."

Murra pursed her lips. They had obviously been planning this for some time. She didn't blame her sister for being ambitious — didn't blame anyone, as long as their ambitions didn't conflict with her own, and there were advantages to working with your family. *"Summer Wife,"* she said meditatively. "Now, that's quite an idea, isn't it?"

"Do you think Blundy would like to do it?" Vincor asked, the eagerness showing in his voice.

"Oh, heavens, Vincor," Murra smiled, "you'd have to ask Blundy about that. I never *interfere*. When you're married to a genius you have to learn to let the man do things his own way." She spread her hands helplessly. Then she said, "Anyway, I think I'll just go up and join them on the ice for a bit; it looks like so much fun."

Before she reached the ice she had to dodge half a dozen screeching pollies, making their escape from Blundy and the little boys. Brightly colored — emerald green, scarlet, one or two patterned with diamonds and polka dots — the pollies weren't dangerous, except to the bugs they fed on, but Murra disliked having them there: they were uncontrolled. Climbing up from the greensward onto the glacier itself was a very un-Murralike thing to do. It meant puffing and panting, and besides the grass turned into mud and the mud into slush before you were on solid ice. She was glad she'd worn old boots.

She was also glad she'd worn warm clothes, because it was *cold* up there. Not winter cold, of course; the sun was still hot. But the breeze was chilling.

Besides, she could hear sounds of running water from underneath the ice, and now and then a sharp cracking sound, like a large stick snapping. Was this place really *safe?*

She paused and looked at Blundy and the two little boys, Petternel the sturdy fourteen-month-old, Porly the toddler. They hadn't seen her yet. They had found a smooth place for sliding, and they were running toward it, then planting their feet and gliding along it, arms windmilling to keep their balance, shouting with pleasure, laughing when little Porly fell down anyway.

It was very good, Murra thought with satisfaction, to see her husband laughing like that again. The picnic had been an excellent idea. She glanced around. The world was a pretty sight from the ice sheet. She could see clear down to Sometimes River and to the dozen streams that fed it with meltwater, some of them crystal clear as the ice itself, some milky white with the powdered rock they had ground away in their course. It would have been even prettier if it were a photograph or a painting hanging in her drawing room, and a lot warmer, she thought, and for a moment wondered if she should try painting again. For a while in the early part of her second year Murra, before she turned to poetry, had thought she had a talent for art. But it had been a lot of hard work, with improvement coming very slowly; and anyway then she met Blundy and found a new career. As his leading lady, of course; there was always a part for her in everything Blundy wrote. More importantly, as his wife.

But a wife could also be a mother to children.

Verla had put that unwelcome idea in her mind, not for the first time. It wasn't a prospect Murra could look forward to: four long months of pregnancy, with your belly swelling and your grace of movement stolen away. Then the pain of parturition. Then the other pain if the baby died —

She shuddered. The trouble was that time was running fast on Murra's biological clock. Your second year was when you had your children if you were intelligent about it, and it was an unfortunate fact that Murra's second year was some time past.

But did she really want to have physical children? Squalling, messy ones? Wasn't it better to have mind-children? Her poems, for instance; weren't those as valuable as *babies?*

But there too the clock was running for Murra. If anyone was ever going to be a poet — a *real* poet, a poet whose work would be admired and cherished by many others than the poet's own husband — this was the time to do that, too, wasn't it?

She turned around, startled. Blundy was approaching with the boys, one on either hand. Grinning, Blundy asked, "Time for lunch yet? I hope Verla brought along dry socks for the kids."

"I'm sure she did," Murra said, and waited for Blundy to drop the children's hands so he could help her down the slippery ice, back to where Megrith had put the chops on the grill and old Vorian was gazing wistfully at the spring — he would not likely see another. Concentrating on her footing, Murra had forgotten about the little boys behind them until she heard her sister scream the toddler's name.

They turned. Little Porly was spread-eagled on the ice, with his brother fearfully tugging at him. "He just fell," Petternel moaned, "but he won't get up."

Then all the adults were racing up the slope, Verla in the lead, Megrith close behind her — transformed instantly from cook to doctor. By the time Murra got to them they had all surrounded the child and Megrith had the boy's head on his crouching knee, lifting an eyelid to peer at the eye. Verla was sobbing and Blundy was swearing to himself.

Then the little boy opened the other eye, and, struggling to get up, began to cry.

Megrith gave a little laugh. "He's all right, Verla. He just fell and it knocked the wind out of him. But now his clothes are all wet...and, oh, hell, can't you smell the chops? They'll be burned black if I don't get back to them!"

The chops, really, were quite all right, and so was the salad, and old Vorian, sampling the bottle of wine he had opened, pronounced it first-rate. So the picnic was a success after all, though Verla was still shaken.

When they had settled down after the meal Murra sat next to her husband, watching the others clean up. Lowering her voice, she said, "Oh, Blundy, Vincor had an idea he wanted to talk over with you. *Summer Wife.* A new series for the hot time; what do you think?"

Blundy pursed his lips. Then he shrugged. But he hadn't said no. "Of course," she went on, "we wouldn't have to have the same cast, exactly, I mean if you think it's worth doing at all. For instance, maybe I'm getting a little too, well, mature for the wife's part — "

And waited for him to say, "That's ridiculous. I wouldn't do anything like that without you, you know that," and found the day quite spoiled for her when he didn't.

Chapter Five

Mercy MacDonald was nothing if not fair, so fair that she even gave Deputy Captain Hans Horeger credit when he earned it — even him. As a human being he was scum and nothing would change her mind about that. Still, she admitted to herself that he was a first-class ship handler. The way he eased *Nordvik* into its capture orbit around Slowyear was optimal. Nothing shuddered or jerked. The thrust just dwindled, and dwindled more, until they were there.

It was the slowest part of the long journey. MacDonald spent it lying in her bed, trying to make herself sleep. She failed. There were too many thoughts and memories and sudden starts of apprehension to wake her right up again every time she came close. They had to do with the decision she would have to make (jump ship or stay?), with the barren wasteland that was her life up to this moment (tedium punctuated with blazing flareups of anger — at, for instance, Hans Horeger) and, most of all, with the worry about what these Slowyear people were going to be like. Would they be friendly? Even welcoming? Would they at least not be unkind?

There were things she had learned about them which were, to say the least, not reassuring. For instance, their criminal law. What kind of human beings punished every infraction of the law with the chance of instant death? What people would simply cut themselves off from communication — however tenuous or difficult, or even pointless — with the rest of the galaxy?

For that matter, what kind of people could go on living in so mean an environment? (And could she herself possibly live as one of them?)

Then the last little gentle nudge of thrust was gone. They had arrived.

It was a critical moment, a moment to reflect, a transitional moment. But there wasn't much chance for reflection. What there was was pandemonium. With *Nordvik* at relative rest, nothing weighed anything anymore and everybody was scurrying around the ship chasing the floating pens, dishes, books, keys — chasing down and capturing the thousand little items that somebody should have secured, but hadn't. They should have remembered what zero thrust was like, of course, but years made you forget even that. What Mercy MacDonald had forgotten was to put the lid on a jar of hard candies. She'd taken them out to have one to suck as a prophylactic against no-weight nausea. Then the whole jarful had followed her out the door and halfway down the hall, bright little balls of colored sugar that were sure to raise hell with the air pumps or the light fixtures if she didn't track them down.

So in that very significant moment all she was seeing of the planet they had come to visit was a quick glimpse out of the corner of her eye now and then.

In fact it didn't look like anything special anyway. It looked a lot like every other habitable planet in the universe, naturally enough. Blue sky, white cloud, dappled land, bright blue seas — that was pretty much what a planet had to look like, if any human being was going to be able to spend much time there. And when she finally got the last peppermint-green candy back in the jar and the lid on tight this time, when she finally was able to race down to the lock room, it didn't look much different even in the big screen.

Except for one thing. It was hard to get a good look at the screen. There was too much in the way. Every one of the fifty-six people of *Nordvik* had huddled there, floating every which way in a thicket of arms and legs and torsos in the microgravity. Still, MacDonald saw the one thing that was different at once. Something new was in the picture. Coming up toward them out of the rim of the planet's dark side was a tiny diamond-bright point of intense white light.

A shuttle was already rising from the planet.

"I told you they'd be eager," Hans Horeger said happily. "See that? They couldn't even wait for us to come down in our own shuttle. They had to launch theirs right away." But then, out of loyalty to the ship, he added, "I'll bet it's a piece of junk, though. A place like this hardly sees a ship every fifty years. We don't want to depend on them." He peered around the crowded lock room for the engineering officer, pushing stray limbs out of his way. "Dave? Is our own shuttle ready?"

It was, of course, and Horeger had known all along that it was, because he'd been driving the poor engineers crazy for a month, testing every circuit to make sure no part of the shuttle had broken or rotted away since the last time they'd used it.

Horeger's wife, hanging on to her husband's shoulder for a better look as the Slowyear shuttle moved closer, said disgustedly, "That's pretty ancient, Hans."

He frowned. "It's bigger than I expected, though. And they're really pouring on the power."

His wife turned her look of disgust to him. "There you go again, worrying," she scolded. "What does it matter if it's big? The important thing is it's old. It's a fossil. I bet no one's visited this place in a good long time."

Old Captain Hawkins cleared his throat. From the wall-hold where he was hanging, he said mildly, "We don't know that. All we know is that nobody's come *back* from it for a long time." But no one listened.

No one listened because they couldn't; his deputy had quelled his wife and begun to shout to everyone in general. "All of you," he cried, "pay attention! Quiet down! Do you all remember what your orders are? Nobody goes down to the surface without my permission! No one's allowed into their shuttle unless I order you there. And when *Nordvik* leaves for its next port of call, no one's going to stay behind unless I say you can — and I won't. Do you all understand that?"

He raked his crew with his eyes, one by one, craning and twisting to make each eye contact. Satisfied, or as satisfied as Hans Horeger ever got, he finished, "And if any of you forget what I'm saying, I promise you I'll make you regret it."

But MacDonald noticed that he didn't say how.

Nordvik was a hundred times the size of the shuttle, but they could feel the whole vast starship shuddering as the Slowyear shuttle nuzzled in. Then there were long seconds of squeaking and rasping while the shuttle's portal seals felt the outlines of *Nordvik's,* and slowly adjusted themselves to fit.

Then the lock opened.

Nordvik's whole crew moved forward as one as the shuttle people pulled themselves in, hand over hand. Through the tangled crowd MacDonald could see clearly enough that they were carrying no weapons. There were only three of them. One was a slim young girl who held a briefcase, the second a tall, lean man who had nothing at all in his hands, the third a squat, good-looking one who held only a flower. The man with the flower peered in, at and around the various faces, in all their angles of presentation, taking his time. Then he settled on Mercy MacDonald. He grinned at her and handed her the flower. "My name's Blundy. Welcome to Slowyear," he said.

The young girl gave him a quick, angry look, then turned it on MacDonald. "Are you the governor?" she demanded.

Her accent was odd, but MacDonald understood her easily enough. "We don't have a governor. I guess you mean the captain. That's him over there on the wall," she said, pointing — to the real captain, of course.

"But I'm his executive, so I'm the one you have to talk to," Horeger said quickly. And belatedly added, "Uh, welcome to Interstellar Ship *Nordvik.*"

The girl bent to her briefcase and pulled out a thick sheaf of papers. The man named Blundy still had his eyes appreciatively on Mercy MacDonald. She stared right back. He was, she thought, the smallest person present — well, the shortest, anyway (though even that was hard to be sure of, with everyone floating in odd directions). There was nothing small about his body, especially the thick muscles in his bare forearms. And his eyes did not leave Mercy MacDonald.

He was *interested,* she thought, liking the fact that he was showing interest, even liking the feelings inside her that came from enjoying it. She was sorry when he turned his gaze to Hans Horeger. "The kind of thing we want — " he began.

"Visas first, Blundy," the girl interrupted. "I've got my orders."

"Sure, Petoyne," the man said indulgently, "but they don't have to have visas until they come down, do they?"

"They're all probably going to want to, won't they? So they have to fill out the forms." She cleared her throat and addressed the group: "On behalf of the governor general, I welcome you all to Slowyear — "

"I already said that, Petoyne," said Blundy.

"I'm saying it *officially.* — And ask that you fill out these forms and sign them. Then we can get on with the business we're all really interested in. Each of you take one, please — have you all got pencils? Well, get some, will you?"

While someone was hurrying away to find things to write with, MacDonald took her eyes off the squat man long enough to read one of the forms. The people of this backwater planet didn't seem to have much regular use for such things, she saw, because these were just photocopied printouts, headed "Planet of Slowyear, Department of Trade and Immigration," with the impromptu look of something somebody had remembered to whomp up at the last minute before *Nordvik* arrived. There was an awful lot of tiny type. When she signed that form she would be relinquishing any claim for liability for almost any kind of ill that might befall her on the surface of the planet or on the way to it — from mechanical failure of the planet's ancient shuttles or their own; from navigation errors; from disease or attack by animals…but there weren't any dangerous animals on Slowyear, Mercy MacDonald knew very well; they must have copied the thing out of an old lawbook. Really, it amused her. She looked up at the girl named Petoyne. "I didn't know you had lawyers on Slowyear," she said.

The Slowyear girl gave her an impatient look. "Did you sign it? All right, you've got your visa. Next!"

And the man named Blundy was saying, "Who's in charge of selling stuff?"

MacDonald raised her hand. "I am. Mercy Mac-Donald. Purser."

He looked at her again. "That's nice," he said, approving. "Then let's find some place where we can go, Mercy MacDonald, so we can talk business."

* * *

Business was business, and this Blundy man didn't waste much time getting down to it. He perched companionably next to her at her display screen, one hand lightly holding her shoulder, and frowned at the readout. No seeds, ova or sperm right now, he said; not on this first trip. "We came up light so we could carry a max load back, so there's no refrigeration on board this time." No living plants right now, either, not until that other man, whose name was Gowen, finished checking them. "He's our health officer," Blundy explained. "He'll stay on board until he quick-cultures everything — so you won't bring anything nasty down with you, you know."

"He's going to check everything? Even us?"

Blundy looked surprised. "Hasn't he done you yet? No, of course not; well, give him a drop of blood as soon as you can. You're coming on the first trip, of course."

"I am?"

Blundy grinned at her. "Of course you are — I'm glad to say. We'll only take two of you this time — to have as much cargo mass as possible, you see — and that deputy captain of yours insists on being one of them. So you're the other."

MacDonald just smiled at that, not having made her own mind up yet — though actually there wasn't any real doubt about it — and he got back to business. Scrimshaw? Sure. A lot of people would like that sort of stuff, he conceded, though only heaven knew why. Books? Certainly; and music and dramas and dance recitals, too, why not?

But the big thing, he told her, was datastores. "Science, history, medicine — *especially* medicine; we'll buy copies of everything you've got about medicine or biochemistry. Diagnosis, therapies, pharmaceuticals, surgical procedures — you name it, we'll buy it. Can you get all that in the first load? I assume all this stuff is electronic, so it won't mass much — Fine! Now, what are these Hades artifacts I see on the list?"

He kept her jumping, but it wasn't all business. She could see that. She didn't miss the way he was looking at her, even when what he was talking about was merchandise. It was exciting.

It gave her pleasure. The excitement was good for her. She could feel it in her groin, an almost sexual tingling — no, she corrected herself fairly, not "almost" at all. It was definitely sexual, all right. And Blundy's interest in her was not just for generic sex, as it always was with dirty Hans Horeger, because when she took the stranger to see Betsy arap Dee she observed carefully that, although he gave Betsy a thoroughly assessing look, his eyes returned to MacDonald herself.

Betsy, of course, assessed him right back. It didn't seem to be serious though because the other stranger, Gowen, had obviously already taken a lien on Betsy's interest when he took her blood sample. The four of them went over Betsy's datastores rapidly, and before they were halfway through MacDonald made a surprising discovery.

The surprise was that Betsy wasn't moping. More than that, for the first time since the death of her baby, Betsy looked not only alert but actually happy. There was no other word for it. Her face flushed and her eyes sparkled; she smiled; she even laughed out loud.

Then MacDonald made the even more surprising discovery that she was quite happy too. She was eager to board the shuttle and find out what this forbidding, but also intriguing, new planet had to offer her.

Of course, that was the point at which Hans Horeger came bustling into the datastore room, radiating officious authority and orders. MacDonald didn't let even that puncture her mood. She let him strut for a few minutes. Then, "Come on, Hans," she said, pulling him by the sleeve as she invented an errand to get him away from Betsy and the new man — realizing with astonishment that it was the first time in a good while that she had deliberately invited Horeger to do anything with her — "come on, help me pick out the first load of scrimshaw and start loading the shuttle."

That kept them both busy for half an hour. Then, with the selections made, she left Horeger to round up a loading crew, shouting more orders that no one either heeded or needed, and she went looking for the "health officer."

He wasn't in the datastore room, wasn't even with Betsy arap Dee, who was back in her own room dreamily changing into more interesting clothes. MacDonald finally found all three of the Slowyear people together, hanging onto wall holds and talking quietly together. For a moment she thought they might not want to be interrupted, but as soon as Blundy caught sight of her he beckoned her over.

"I thought you could take my blood sample now," she explained to Gowen, holding out her wrist. The girl, Petoyne, sniffed at that, but Gowen immediately dug into his pouch and pulled out a tiny syringe. It didn't hurt. It only took a second — long enough to pull a thin streak of red into an ampoule — but also long enough for Petoyne to turn away in a marked manner and leave.

"Gowen'll put your sample in a culture box," Blundy explained. "By the time we land we'll know for sure if you have to go into quarantine or anything. But you look pretty healthy to me."

She smiled back at him, but said, "Are you sure I should go on the first trip? That girl didn't look as though she wanted me to."

"Oh," he said dismissively, "*Petoyne*. Don't worry about Petoyne. Pack a bag, and don't be too long, please — you don't want to miss the flight!"

She didn't, though. Didn't pack just one bag; at least, did pack one, and then bit her thumb for a moment, and went on to pack a second, and a third, until everything she really wanted to preserve of all her life to date was packed.

It took up more space in the shuttle than she had planned, but Blundy only grinned and, although Hans Horeger certainly saw it and was not pleased at all, his wife, who was complaining about being left on the ship, was a more immediate problem for him. And then they were inside, and the hatches were closed, and they were on their way.

Chapter Six

Not even Murra stayed home on the day the first shuttle came back from the ship. She dressed herself in her prettiest robes and perfumed herself with an extra bit of her special (if no longer unique) essence, since she would be outdoors. Before leaving the house she studied herself in the mirror for several minutes. Then, regretfully, she took off the pretty bugsilk slippers that became her feet so well and replaced them with sheepskin half-boots. The boots were beautifully ornamented of course, but so *rugged*. She didn't have any choice about that. Practicality had to triumph over looks because, even though warmspring had begun to dry out the landscape, there would surely be mud and puddles near the landing strip.

There were. She was lucky enough to get a ride up the slope on a flatbed. Although it was packed she wasn't refused, since everyone was kind enough to make room for Blundy's Murra. The landing strip was on the far side of the pass, five kilometers of meadow bulldozed flat, and at least five thousand other people had already gathered there. Scores of armbanded marshals were herding them behind a roped line away from the strip itself, but even the marshals were looking up half the time in the hope of catching a glimpse of a shuttle through the clouds. Heaven knew how many thousand others were up in the hills, watching with binoculars or simply their unaided eyes. Everybody was bouncing with anticipation. Children ran and shouted. Vendors were all through the crowd, selling cold drinks and sandwiches.

There was a scream from the sky. Five thousand heads jerked back, and voices began to shout: "I see it. There it is! It's coming!"

Then, squinting, Murra saw it too — first the thread-thin snowy plume that followed the shuttle, then the glint of the spacecraft itself. It was high overhead, passing beyond them to the east, then banking sharply and turning back.

When at last it landed Murra thought she had never seen anything moving so fast — as indeed she hadn't; it was going a good hundred and fifty kilometers an hour, even with its flaps and airbrakes extended. But it settled on the strip cleverly enough, though sudden spurts of smoke and dust puffed up as its tires touched. It rolled away, long away — far down the strip, until it was only a toylike thing.

Then the marshals gave up trying to keep order. The crowds burst through, running toward the shuttle. At the end of the strip a waiting tractor backed itself into position to snag the towring in the shuttle's nose and begin to drag it back toward the sheds.

Murra spared herself that silly scramble. She knew perfectly well that it would be nearly half an hour before the shuttle was in position and had cooled off enough for the hatches to be opened. She waited. She planted herself where the movable stairs were ready to be rolled into position, bought an ice from a vendor — who almost forgot to take her money, she was so intent on staring down the runway — and allowed the whole procession to come to her. When everybody had come drifting back, pacing the slowly dragged shuttle itself, Murra was in the front row, neatly finishing the last of her ice.

Even then, even there, nearly everybody recognized Murra. While they waited for the shuttle to finish its cooling process, crackling and pinging alarmingly as it did, people took time to smile at her, and nod. She accepted their attention as graciously as always. It didn't particularly please her; it simply would have puzzled her if it had been withheld. When at last the handlers pushed the rolling stairs to the hatch and it opened Murra did not join in the cheering. She was there, though. She was right there to see Blundy and Petoyne appear in the doorway with a couple of strangers, strutty little man and dark middle-aged woman; and she only had to see the woman once to see what she saw. As soon as they came down she was right at the foot of the stairs gracefully moving up between the woman and Blundy to kiss him. "I'm so glad to have you back, my very dearest," she said, marking out her claim, "and I hope you've remembered to invite your friends to dine with us tomorrow night. Her too," she said, gazing benignly at Petoyne.

Murra saw rather little of her husband that day, or at least not at close range. He was frequently on the news screen, of course: taking the visitors to see the governor, showing the visitors around the summer city, standing with the visitors as they were welcomed, and welcomed, and welcomed. No, actually she saw quite a lot of Blundy that day, and it pleased her that she saw him as she did because so did everyone else on Slowyear.

It was less pleasing, though, because it was never Blundy alone she saw on the screen but always Blundy plus that foolish little Petoyne, and Blundy with that rather unattractive starship woman who would, Murra was resignedly certain, be the next Petoyne in Blundy's life…for a time.

By the time Blundy got home that night he was too tired to talk, or said he was. She had expected as much. Anyway, as she certainly had expected, he slept that night where he belonged, next to her side. He didn't talk in the morning, either, because as soon as he was awake he was out, muttering excuses, no time, so much to do; but that was all right, too, because the dinner was a fixture for that night.

In a whole marriage's worth of arranging pleasing dinners for Blundy she was determined this would be the grandest and best. Everything would have to be perfect; so to begin with Murra called in the cleaners as soon as he was out of the house, and informed her cooker that he would be needed by noon at the latest to start preparing the meal. Then, content that that much was well in hand, she allowed herself to go shopping.

The shopping was for food, she told herself. But although there were plenty of food stores nearer than the central marketplace, that was where she went. That was where everyone else went, too, because the second shuttle, this one the starship's own, had landed at daybreak, and the people from the ship were already setting up their displays.

Of course, there weren't any actual *goods* there; those were already in the sheds by the landing strip. What the ship people had were a dozen or so video displays to show the catalogue of their wares. One screen was showing a succession of industrial-looking machines, another household appliances, a third plants of many kinds, from tiny baby's breath blossoms to giant redwoods, a fourth animals. It was hard to see individuals in the press around the displays, but a short, sallow man stranger at one of the booths came forward to greet her. "Mrs., ah, Blundy, isn't it?" he asked, and she recognized the man she had invited to dinner.

"Actually my name is Murra. I'm afraid I didn't catch yours?"

"Hans Horeger," the man said promptly, holding out his hand. "I'm executive officer and deputy captain — acting captain, really," he said, with a deprecating shrug, "because old Hawkins is really pretty much past it."

"I'm honored," Murra said gravely. "And please do be sure to come tonight, and bring your charming friend — "

"You mean Mercy MacDonald, I suppose," Horeger said. Murra was aware of his eyes on her, missing nothing. His study of her was discreet, which she appreciated, but also quite admiring, which she appreciated even more. "Would you call her charming? I guess so, in her way — but of course next to someone like you — "

She gave him her prettiest smile. "I don't see her here," she remarked, looking around.

The man looked around too. "No, I guess she's not back yet. She and your husband had to go to the sheds to look at some samples."

She nodded. "Yes," she said, "I rather thought they would."

Blundy and herself, the two from the starship, Petoyne — there had to be one more, a male, to make an even number. Since the extra male would be more or less Petoyne's escort, he needn't be particularly attractive. Murra thought for a moment, then smiled and picked up the phone. It was answered at once. "Vorian? I know how much you wanted to meet the people from the starship. Well, if you're free for dinner this evening — "

Of course he was. That settled, Murra gave orders and watched until she was sure the cleaner and the cooker were well started on them. Normally Murra didn't care for hired servants. But they were absolutely necessary this night, for there would be no spending time in the kitchen for the hostess. When she was convinced they were properly doing the gruntwork they were hired for, Murra began doing the things she alone could do. She arranged the flowers she had bought prettily around the room. Then music: She selected tapes of unobtrusive strings and flutes to play in the background. Then she programmed the big wall screen with suitable background images, mostly a series of still shots from *Winter Wife* and other productions she and Blundy had done together, with, of course the most flattering shots of herself featured. She worked as hard as the hired help, because it all had to be perfect....

It *was* perfect, too. She was sure of that before the first guest arrived. Yet when Mercy MacDonald showed up Murra had a quick moment of doubt. The woman had managed to get herself rested and cleaned up, and she did not look quite so middle-aged anymore. Indeed, Murra thought justly, she looked no older than herself. She greeted the woman with a hands-on-the-shoulder almost hug, and gave the air by her ear an almost kiss. "We're so grateful you took the time to come, my dear," she said, sweetly and intimately, as though they had been long-lost sisters, tragically separated somehow but still, somehow, bonded for life. "Oh, what's this? You shouldn't have." For the woman was handing her something soft wrapped in an even softer fabric. Was it bugsilk? No, Murra realized, it had to be *real* silk! From old Earth! It was a pity that it was patterned with those quite hideous flowers, but still. One day, Murra thought — but not a very near day, not until the woman who had given it to her was no longer around — that wrapping could become a pretty scarf, or something attractively unusual to throw over the back of a chair.

When she unwrapped it and saw what the wrapping contained she said warmly, "Why, it's really *beautiful,*" trying not to laugh, but all the same making sure Blundy saw with what effort she was politely not laughing. The gift inside was — imagine! — a stiff piece of some coarse fabric sewn with wool lettering. *Greetings from space,* it said, in strident green, blue, and purple.

"It's a sampler. People on Earth used to make them to hang up in their living rooms," Mercy MacDonald explained. "I didn't know if you'd like it — we call this sort of thing scrimshaw. People on other planets like to have these things, for souvenirs of our visit."

"It's stunning," Murra said, knowing that Blundy would understand she thought it hideous; and just because she thought it so hideous she insisted that Blundy put it up at once on the wall over the couch in the living room.

"Can't I help?" the man from the ship asked politely.

"Of course not, Captain Horeger," Murra said warmly, consciously flattering him by upgrading his title. "You're a guest."

"Oh, please, call me Hans," he said, looking at her with admiration, and not bothering to mention the fact that Mercy MacDonald, who was also a guest, was already standing to help Blundy with the hanging.

"Hans, then," she said, saying it in a way that conveyed appreciation of the name, and also of the man who owned it. "Please, just sit down and make yourself comfortable. Let me get you some wine? It's summer wine from last year. That's when the grapes are best, just when everything starts to get too hot to grow." And smiled at him while she was pouring, but did not fail to see, out of the corner of her eye, Mercy MacDonald handing the sampler up to Blundy, and their hands touching.

* * *

Although there were only six at dinner it wasn't quite as intimate as Murra had intended. Though only the six of them sat down to eat, Rosha, the cleaner, had stayed on to serve and Grannis, the cooker, insisted on carrying some of the dishes in himself, thrilled to be so close to the visitors; and both of them felt quite free to take part in the conversation.

Murra made sure there was plenty of conversation, careful to guide it to new areas whenever it showed signs of slowing (after all, Murra's dinners were not about food, they were about *talk.*) But it didn't need much guiding. There was plenty to talk about. The visitors had so much to learn about Slowyear, and the locals were delighted to tell them. About Slowyear's seasons: "Well, yes, we have a very long year," Blundy was telling Mercy MacDonald, "so we divide it into six principal seasons — coldspring, warmspring, summer, hotfall, coldfall, and, of course, winter."

Petoyne made a face. "Winter's the worst," she said, looking at Mercy MacDonald in a very wintery way.

"Not for me," Rosha disagreed. He leaned past Murra to set down the soup tureen. "Wow, that was heavy," he informed them all. "The way I look at it, when it's winter at least you can dress warm and go out for a little while if you want to, but there's nowhere to go in summer. Unless you're rich. How's the soup?"

"Fine," Blundy said, just as though it were a reasonable question for a server to ask.

"Good, I'll tell Grannis," he said, and reluctantly left the room.

Murra smiled after him, just as though she meant it. "As a matter of fact," she told her guests, "Blundy and I do go to one of the polar places sometimes in the summer." Then she saw the look on Blundy's face. "But not this one, I think," she said.

Blundy picked up the conversation where it had been interrupted. "So altogether we have a hundred months, each one about seventy days long — there are holidays now and then to make it come out even with the year. Right now we're in Green, coming up on Flower. The whole countryside gets really pretty in Flower; you'd like it."

"I was born in Flower," Vorian contributed. "That isn't a good time, though. I was just beginning to get big enough to be really active when summer came along. My mother told me she had the devil of a time keeping me indoors from Fry to Sweat."

"And I was born on the sixty-seventh of Shiver — that's the first month of winter," Murra added, "and Blundy's birthday is the forty-fifth of Christmas, while Petoyne here has just had her very first birthday. The 11th of Green, wasn't it, dear?"

Petoyne looked down at her food without answering. Blundy took up the thread. "So I'm two and seventeen months," he told the company. "That would be about thirty-five of your years, Mercy. And, let's see, Murra's now — "

Murra was already overriding his voice. To the deputy captain: "Are you really enjoying your soup?"

"It's delicious," Horeger responded gallantly. "What is it?"

Petoyne giggled. "You don't want to know. What do you eat on the ship?"

"Nothing as good as this," Horeger said at once, and gave Murra a complimentary smile. She smiled back, comfortably aware that the main appreciation in his eyes was not for the food but for herself. That was a situation familiar to Murra, and always welcome. There was no doubt in her mind that this Hans Horeger person would sooner or later do his best to get her alone, and from there to a bed. She didn't mind that. She looked forward to it, in fact. She also, however, knew that she definitely would not let it go that far, not ever. The self-indulgence of actually sleeping with any of the men who had made it clear she was invited would cost too much. At a minimum, it would mean the sacrificing of a grievance: she wouldn't be un-selfishly tolerating Blundy's adulteries anymore. Simply knowing that she could easily be bedded by Horeger was almost as good as doing it, and a lot less trouble in the long run.

When the scoggers were served, and each of the guests from the spaceship had sampled them with enjoyment, Petoyne spoke up. "They're bugs, you know," she said, avoiding Murra's quick vexed look. "The soup was made out of their shells, now this is the meat."

Horeger stopped with a fork almost to his lips. "Bugs?"

Blundy took over, explaining that Slowyear's na-tive fauna were seldom vertebrate, not counting the flying "pollies," and never mammalian. The largest life forms the original settlers found were arthropods, vaguely like terrestrial insects, with an insectoid egg-pupa-winged life cycle. "You won't see them now — they're only out at night — but they're around," he told the visitors. "Then when the dry season starts they burrow into the ground and cocoon up. In hotfall they come out when the rains start. By then they're big winged things the size of my fist; they fly, eat, mate, lay eggs, and die. Then the eggs hatch and over the winter the pupae grow underground. We use dogs to dig them up in the winter, before they hatch out by themselves; this time of year we can catch them on the surface, if we're good at it."

"These are fresh," Murra said, proudly careful to refrain from displaying the pride she felt in the meal she had set before her guests — after all, not every hostess could provide out-of-season delicacies on short notice. "Hunters brought them back this morning."

"They do taste good," Horeger said, doubtful but game.

Mercy MacDonald said, "Oh, God, Hans, why shouldn't they? After all, back on Earth we used to eat lobsters. We'd eat them on the ship, too, if we had any."

Which led to talk about shiplife. That was the part that really fascinated the servers, consequently slowing the meal down. Murra sighed and resigned herself: at least that meant more time for conversation. Mercy MacDonald described the universal shipboard practice of making scrimshaw — "to sell, sure, but mostly to give us something to do. Otherwise we'd all go crazy." Hans Horeger modestly explained the difficulties involved in guiding a starship across the long light-years between worlds. MacDonald pointed out how boring it was for everyone and how, no matter how

careful they were in dealing with each other, sometimes some members of the crew simply could not
stand some other member of the crew one second
longer — she was, Murra thought with interest, talking
more to her deputy captain than to her hosts. But
Horeger didn't appear to notice. He blithely began to
explain that they would soon have to dislodge the
ship's fuel storage, converting it to a factory for more
fuel and sending it close in to the star for solar energy
to make the antimatter fuel. Murra said quickly,
"Surely there's no hurry. Aren't we being good hosts
for you here?"

"Well," said Hans Horeger, turning toward her, "in
some ways extremely good."

"He means we don't have any complaints at all,"
Mercy MacDonald put in. "You've been so good about
commercial dealings you've just about put me out of
a job. I don't have to bargain! You pay us so well that
we can afford just about everything we ask for —
machine parts, metal, supplies — "

"Some of us can still hope for more," Horeger
murmured in Murra's ear.

"We're getting plenty from you people in return, of
course," Blundy declared, paying no attention to what
was going on at the other end of the table. "That's what
makes good business, a fair price both ways and
everybody sat — Is that the phone, Murra?"

It was. She looked resignedly amused. "Excuse
me, please," she said, getting up. "It won't take me
more than a minute — "

In fact, it took less. She wasn't out of the dining
room before Grannis appeared from the kitchen, his

flushed face looking sad. "Say, Murra," he said, "this isn't so good. It's your sister. You know your nephew Porly? She says he's in the hospital."

While Murra was out of the room everybody, of course, had some sort of reassurance, or at least good wishes, to offer. But it was Horeger who said the thing that no one else said. He looked around the table, then turned to Blundy. "Is it this infant-mortality thing you people have?" he asked.

Vorian gave him a sharp look. "What infant-mortality thing is that?" he demanded.

Horeger looked surprised. "Oh, shouldn't I have said anything? I mean, I wondered why you were so hot for all our medical data and so on, so I assumed that was it. All the babies that die, I mean."

"Who told you about babies dying?" Vorian asked, but Blundy answered instead.

"What difference does it make who told him?" he asked reasonably. "That's right, Horeger. We have a very high infant-mortality rate; it's the worst thing about living here. And every time a ship comes by we hope they'll have something we can use — but they never have so far."

"I thought so," Horeger said, sounding satisfied. "Believe me, Blundy, we want to help you any way we can — "

"Oh, Christ," Mercy MacDonald interrupted him. "Why don't you just shut up?"

Horeger turned a wrathful face on her. "Have you forgotten who you're talking to?" His voice was strangled, as though he was striving against insuperable odds for self-control. "I'm simply making a humanitarian offer of aid to people in need."

"Yes? What kind of aid is that? We don't even have a real doctor on *Nordvik*." She looked at Blundy. "I think," she said, "the best thing we could do is mind our business."

Vorian sighed. "We'd appreciate that," he said softly. "And now I think it's getting late for an old man to be out."

When Murra came back they were all at the door, and unwilling to be cajoled into staying. "No, really," Horeger said apologetically, pressing her hand. "We really must go. Especially you, Mercy."

MacDonald gave him a surprised look. "Me?"

Horeger nodded blandly. "To catch the shuttle back to *Nordvik*," he explained. "It'll be taking off early in the morning and you'll have to be on it."

"I will?"

"It's your job." He was grinning at her, but quite determined. "You have to check out the rest of the cargo. Oh, you can come back down when that's done, of course."

MacDonald thought for a moment, then shrugged. "I'll do that," she said. "Good night, Murra."

And then all the good nights were said. It was too bad in a way, Murra thought, that Verla's call about little Porly had spoiled the party. On the other hand, one major part of the party's purpose had been to allow Blundy the chance to compare his wife and the challenging new woman side by side. Murra was quite content with the results.

Blundy offered to show Horeger and MacDonald back to the quarters they had been given, with the rest of *Nordvik's* landing party. Vorian went along. But when Petoyne started to leave with them, Murra touched her arm in a friendly way. "Stay a little, please?" she urged. "I sent the servers home, so could you help me straighten things up?"

Petoyne couldn't refuse that, as Murra had intended she couldn't; and when, sulkily, the child began to pick up glasses to take them to the housework room, Murra stopped her. "The cleaner will be back tomorrow to take care of that," she said sweetly. "Sit down, Petoyne. Help me finish that last bottle of wine — you're old enough now, surely. Just sit with me a minute, please."

Petoyne was unwilling, but she was also very young. She did as she was told by the older woman whose husband she had borrowed. She watched without speaking while Murra fetched clean glasses from the sideboard and poured, chatting idly about the soup, that awful "scrimshaw" thing, the guests.

"I'm sorry about your nephew," Petoyne offered.

Murra looked surprised, then shrugged. "It's a pity, of course, but what can you do?" She sipped her wine, looking at Petoyne over the top of her glass. "You know, you've been very brave."

Petoyne stiffened. "Me? Brave?"

"I don't know what else to call it. I know this is difficult for you, dear," Murra said, her tone sympathetic. "It's an unfortunate situation. Blundy is a wonderful man, but he simply can't help being drawn to attractive women."

Petoyne, with her untouched wine glass before her, said stiffly, "If you're talking about Mercy MacDonald, I don't have anything to be brave about. I happen to know Blundy and that woman aren't lovers. Blundy would have told me."

"No, I don't suppose they are, now," Murra agreed. "But they surely will be, dear, and you mustn't let yourself be hurt."

Petoyne looked at her for a moment without speaking. Then she stood up, proud if young. "I'll be all right, Murra. I do want to go home now."

"Of course," Murra smiled, and would have kissed her cheek at the door if the girl had given her a chance. She gazed after her, quite content. They all had to learn, after all. These little peccadillos of Blundy's were — well — sometimes hard to accept, as no one knew better than she. In the long run they didn't matter, for what was certain was that such silly affairs were all temporary and in any case definitely did not threaten Blundy's marriage to Murra. Sooner or later they always would end — this one with the woman from the interstellar ship sooner than most, of course.

And, she thought, heading back into the house, it was an established fact that Blundy *never* went back to a previous mistress. Poor starship woman. Poor Petoyne.

Chapter Seven

When Mercy MacDonald pulled herself out of the shuttle into *Nordvik's* hatch the first thing that struck her was how many people there were aboard the old ship, and how few of them she knew. The only one nearby was not one she really wanted to talk to, but she did her best to be amenable. "Hello, Maureen," she said to Horeger's wife, who was looking even sulkier than usual.

The woman grunted. "So how's Slowyear?" she asked, managing to convey in three words her extreme irritation at not having already seen it for herself.

"It's fine. You'll like it," MacDonald said generously. "Do you know where Betsy arap Dee is?"

"Christ, no. I don't know where anybody is," Maureen Horeger complained. "You could try the datastore room — unless she's shacked up with that damn Slowyear doctor again."

"Thanks," MacDonald said, quite pleased at the news. And when she found Betsy, in the datastore room after all, she was even more pleased to see the sparkle in her friend's eyes. The health officer from Slowyear that, MacDonald supposed, had put it there wasn't with her, but old Captain Hawkins was. So MacDonald didn't think it the right time to ask the questions on her mind, although she was pretty sure she knew the answers anyway. "Horeger," she said, "wants the complete manifest brought up to date, and I'm supposed to check it out. Can you help me?"

"No problem," Betsy said cheerfully, but the old captain had ideas of his own for MacDonald's time. He was, it turned out, looking for warm bodies to help prepare the drive unit for its remote-controlled sojourn near the star, soaking up solar energy to make antimatter fuel. "What do you mean, you can't, Mercy?" he complained. "But most of the crew's already down on Slowyear! I want to go there myself."

"That's fine," she said, slightly surprised. "Come down with me; I'll be going back as soon as I can."

"I wish! But I've got to finish my work here." He gave her an eager look. "I get the impression you're enjoying Slowyear," he said. "How are things going?"

"My God, wonderful. They're buying everything, and they don't care what it costs."

He said wistfully, "You know, maybe we could buy what we need to fix the ship up after all. I've got to get down there and see — only how am I supposed to get them started on the fuel production, so I can get away?"

"Draft some of these new people," she suggested. There were certainly plenty of them. *Nordvik* had more people aboard it than it had seen in years, and three-quarters of them were Slowyearians. They were all over the old ship, poking into crew quarters, looking into storage holds, grinning (or politely trying not to grin) at the sanitary facilities (of course micro-gravity made all that sort of thing much more compli-cated; the toilets worked better when the ship was underway), taking pictures of the bridge — when Mercy MacDonald opened the door of her own room, there was even a Slowyearian in her bed, blinking up at her in surprise, the covers pulled around her head. "Oh," the woman in the bed said, "you must be the one — your name is — oh, hell," she said finally, beginning to unbuckle the sleep straps, "this is your room, isn't it? I'm sorry. I didn't know you were coming back. Look, I'll get right out of here; just give me a minute to get my clothes on."

She was floating free in the room, scrabbling in total non-dignity for the handhold she had forgotten to grasp, before MacDonald could stop her. She was also quite naked. MacDonald found herself laughing. "But it's really all right," she said to the naked woman. "Stay where you are. Please. I'm just coming up to get a few more things and I'm going to catch the next shuttle back down."

The woman looked at her, still half asleep. "You're sure you don't mind?" Then she realized she had nothing on and made a grab for a sheet. Fortunately she caught a flying corner and managed to tug herself back to the bed. Wrapped in the sheet, now firmly holding to the grip of the headboard, she joined MacDonald in laughing. "Sorry about all this," she said again. "Look, I'm Ilson. Burganjee Ilson Threely." She held out a hand and MacDonald drifted herself close enough to shake it.

"Mercy MacDonald," Mercy MacDonald said, releasing the hand. "Why don't you stay right where you are? It won't take me more than ten minutes to get everything together — there's not that much here that I want to keep — and then you can go back to sleep."

"Fine," Ilson said, and watched silently for a moment while MacDonald opened closets, pulled out drawers, searched through cabinets. She had pretty well cleaned her stuff out, but there were, she found, a few bits of clothes, plus a few keepsakes, she had overlooked. She threw everything into a cloth bag, closing the top every time to keep what she packed from drifting out again. "You look like you're getting ready for a long stay," Ilson offered.

"Um," MacDonald said, bobbing her head but more interested in the cabinet she was ransacking.

"I guess it makes a nice change," Ilson said sociably. "It does for me. Being here on this ship, I mean. I'm an instrument and control device specialist; I never though I'd have the chance to actually study a spaceship's systems."

"Are you getting all the help you need?" MacDonald said, making the effort to be polite.

"Oh, sure, everybody's been great. It's not that hard, anyway. This ship's a pretty standard design — for the old days, I mean. I could probably fly it myself."

That made MacDonald look at her more closely. Why would this sensible-looking woman want to know how to fly an interstellar ship? Slowyear didn't have any. Slowyear wasn't going to be building any, either, certainly not in the lifetime of anyone alive there now. They couldn't. They didn't have any of the necessary resource base: they had no antimatter technology, no *c*-speed instruments, none of the complicated gadgetry you needed to get a ship from star to star.

So, MacDonald deduced, there could be only one reason for Ilson's interest: the woman was intending to ship out on *Nordvik* when it left.

There was a lot that Mercy MacDonald could have said to this woman. She didn't say any of it. The regrettably bad decisions of a Slowyearian woman she didn't even know were none of MacDonald's business, and she wanted to get everything done that she needed to do on *Nordvik* so she wouldn't miss her shuttle. She threw the last decent blouse she owned into the bag, closed it, held herself steady with one hand to the doorknob, her brow wrinkled as she tried to remember if there was anything else worth taking. Then she shrugged and said, "I guess that's it." She was silent for a moment, looking around the room. "I wonder if I'll miss this place," she mused out loud.

Ilson looked surprised. "Then you *are* planning to stay on Slowyear for a while," she said.

"You bet. For the rest of my life," said Mercy MacDonald with satisfaction. "So I make you a present of this room. May it give you more pleasure than it ever gave me."

Chapter Eight

In a way, Blundy wasn't sorry that Mercy MacDonald was back on the ship for a few days, or at least not entirely sorry. (He did feel strongly that there was unfinished business between them, and since she was just off a ship that business couldn't be postponed too long.) He had work to do, though, by which he meant not the creation of silly entertainments that other people valued so but his *real* work. Politics.

He faced the fact that, at present, his most effective political work had to be non-political. That was because that was the non-political present mood of the people of Slowyear, who could never (Blundy believed) keep more than one thought in their minds at a time. Right now what obsessed all minds was the ship; so Blundy gave up the idea of proposing taxtime reforms and building programs and concentrated on making sure that whenever anyone thought of *Nordvik* and its crew they also had to think about Arakaho Blundy Spenotex as well.

Meanwhile there was a job to be done that was sort of political. The governor and the council had invited a few prominent persons, Blundy one of them, to help them deal with the trade problem.

That wasn't too tough, except that they should have taken care of all that long since — trade had already begun. There wasn't any doubt of that, because from the window of the council room, where they had gathered, they could look right down on the marketplace and see the shopping going on.

So they disposed of it quickly. They already had Mercy MacDonald's catalogue of the goods *Nordvik* wanted to sell them. All they had to do was make a generous estimate of their aggregate value, then double it, then issue enough supplementary scrip to divide among the people of Slowyear to pay for it all. The only hard part was allocating the proper amount of scrip to each citizen, because the governor thought the most important citizens should be awarded extra scrip, and some of the council put forth the idea that lawbreakers, for instance, should be given less. But Blundy argued for flat-equal distribution to every living human on Slowyear, babies and felons included. He carried the day.

"After all," the governor mused when the vote had been taken, consoling himself for the defeat, "what does it matter? The only thing that's important is to make the ship people happy."

And one of the council, shrewdly looking forward to future power changes, said, "Exactly. We'll call it the Blundy plan, and we can start the distribution tomorrow."

All that went just as Blundy wished it, but he was dissatisfied. He began to wish for Mercy MacDonald's return. Not just for her physical company, although there was certainly a sexual interest, but for what she knew. In Blundy's eyes, Mercy MacDonald was a resource. She had once lived on Earth. Earth was the breeding ground of all politics, and he yearned to ask her for everything she knew.

Where MacDonald was, however, was two hundred-odd kilometers overhead, circling Slowyear nineteen times a day. Twice, after dark, he looked up and was able to pick out the glimmer of *Nordvik* in its angled orbit. There were shuttles going back and forth, almost every day. There wasn't any shortage of ship people. More than thirty of them had already come down in one shuttle or another — even in *Nordvik's* own shuttle, time-scarred and reentry-heat stained from its long use in so many different parts of the galaxy. (Slowyearians laughed at it — among themselves; they would not be so rude to their guests.) Almost all of the thirty-odd — always excepting Mercy MacDonald — were still on the surface of Slowyear, being feted and entertained by (and entertaining) their hosts.

Blundy did not fail to note that in one particular place there especially was no shortage of ship people, or at least of one ship person. That place was in his own house. It seemed to Blundy that every time he came home Hans Horeger was there before him, sitting under that dumb piece of scrimshaw on the wall, sipping wine with Murra and looking ill at ease when Murra's husband turned up.

That wasn't important, either. It certainly didn't cause Blundy very much annoyance — least of all, jealousy; if there was anything Blundy was sure of, it was that, whatever Horeger was hoping for in his persistent attentions to Murra, Murra was not supplying it.

But still.

Blundy found himself staying out of the house even more than usual. Fortunately he had a lot to keep him busy. He had nearly decided — at least, he had come to the point of thinking seriously about whether he was going to decide — that it would be worth his political while to write something, after all, about *Nordvik* and its crew, and so he spent a lot of time visiting ("interviewing" was too strong a word) the ship people on Slowyear. That was easy. They were all over, mingling with the natives, looking at everything, curious about everything. They seemed to be happy that the Slowyearians were spending their new scrip freely, snapping up almost everything they had to offer without much regard to price — or quality, either, because a lot of the junk *Nordvik* had hauled from star to star really was junk: old machines that nobody would dream of using anymore, "art" that was almost as ugly as Mercy MacDonald's guest gift, plants that wouldn't grow on Slowyear and sperm and ova of animals that would certainly die there.

None of them were MacDonald, though. When Blundy, tiring of their company decided to go back home for lunch it wasn't to see whether Horeger was there before him.

But of course Horeger was. The only surprising thing was that he wasn't alone. Their doctor, Megrith, was there, and he looked solemn.

Horeger was looking solemn, too, and even Murra seemed sober. Blundy guessed the reason. "Porly?" he asked, and Megrith nodded.

"He's dying, yes."

"But let's not talk about it," Murra said — as she naturally would, since such subjects as the death of a small child were not only depressing but quite a bore.

Horeger, however, wasn't smart enough to let it go. He said, sounding sad and sincere, "I feel we've let you down, Blundy. I wish we'd had something that helped."

Murra started to speak, then restrained herself. "I'll see how lunch is getting on," she said, getting up.

Megrith responded for all of them. "Well, you didn't," he said. "I checked everything in your file myself. Nothing that seems to help with our own situation. Of course, there are plenty of items from way back on Earth. We found entries about all kinds of human prion diseases — kuru, Creutzfeldt-Jakob disease, Gerstmann-Straussler syndrome — and the veterinary syndromes, scrapie and bovine spongiform encephalopathy, but it's all old, old stuff. Our own particular variation of the prion syndrome evidently didn't occur on Earth."

"Maybe not on any other planet we visited, either," Horeger said regretfully, "because we dumped most of their data in, too. Where is he?" When Blundy blinked at him, he added, "Porly, I mean. The baby that is, ah, passing away."

"Oh. In the hospital, of course."

"That's in the winter city," Megrith explained. "The hospital's too much trouble to move with the seasons, with all the equipment and everything. We have aid stations out here, but the real hospital's in the winter city, up under the hill."

"I'd like to see that too," Horeger said thoughtfully. "The whole idea of everybody holing up for the cold weather—that's interesting." Then, looking at Blundy, he added, "Mercy would, too. She's coming back down tomorrow, by the way."

"How very nice," Murra said, coming in to announce lunch and speaking for Blundy without looking at him. "Why don't we all go up there and show you around?"

"I'd love it," Horeger said, moving toward the table. "I'm sure Mercy would, too. And oh," he said, sniffing appreciatively, "that does smell good! What is it? Or shouldn't I ask?"

Blundy didn't have to invite Mercy MacDonald to tour the winter city. Murra did that for him. As soon as the ship woman had returned to the surface Murra was there at the landing strip, welcoming her back warmly, telling her how much pleasure it would give her and Blundy to show Murra and Hans Horeger around the underground dwellings. MacDonald looked at her strangely, but accepted at once; and the next morning they set out up the hill, all four of them in a tractor cab.

The winter city was set into the side of Winter Hill — "Well, what else would we call it?" Murra said, amused. "Regard it well. It's where we all live, squeezed in on top of each other, for ten long months every year."

Horeger stared up at the thirty-meter metal tower on top of Winter Hill. "In that? That big metal thing?"

Murra smiled, and Blundy explained, "The tower is just the entrance. The city's all underground, to conserve heat."

Horeger frowned up at the tower. "But it's got all those doors," he said, as of course it had: six great doors, one at each level, of which only the lowest one was open.

"Because of the snow," Blundy said. "It piles up all winter long, you see. It doesn't start to melt until New Year's, so sometimes it gets twenty meters deep here. As it keeps building up we have to switch to a higher door every month or two so as to come out on top of it."

He halted the tractor at the base of the tower and they got out to look around. Holding her floppy hat against the hilltop breeze, Murra pointed south. "Can you see the pastures over the rim hills there? That's where we take the sheep to fatten; Blundy can tell you all about that."

"Yes," Blundy said, giving his wife a look, "I do go out with the sheep sometimes. It's taxtime work for me. See, we have to pay part of our taxes in community labor, and — "

But, smiling, Horeger was holding up a hand to stop him. "Yes, I know about taxtime. Murra has explained it all."

"Well, anyway.... I pay the taxes that way because I like it. It gives me a chance to be off by myself — "

"Or with a good friend," Murra put in amiably.

"Or with a friend, maybe, but pretty much by myself. So I can think. As a matter of fact," he added,

"I've decided to go out again with the next flock, maybe in a couple of days." He didn't meet the gaze his wife turned on him, but waved to the planted lands down the hill. "That's all farm. We're lucky with our farmland here. We always get good crops; there aren't any native pests, just a few stowaway bugs that sneaked in from Earth on the first landing, and not many of those."

Horeger said, as a pleasantry, "I hope we haven't brought any new ones."

"There's no chance of that," Murra said reassuringly, "because of course we checked everything. Did you know that we have farms in the winter city, too?"

"Under*ground?*" Horeger said in admiration.

"Well, hothouses, anyway," Murra amended herself. "They aren't very big. There's plenty of power and water for them, of course, but we are a little cramped for space. Still, we get fresh vegetables from them all winter long."

"Some," Blundy said.

Murra gave him another look. "Well, we can't grow enough to feed everybody all the time, of course, but there's always plenty of summer-grown food in the freezers."

"The power's the big thing," Blundy said. He took Mercy MacDonald's arm and pointed. "Look over here. Do you see that field that looks like it's just been plowed? It hasn't been. They're solar collectors. They're where we get most of our heat and power. Murra can tell you all about that; she works there."

"Just for taxtime," Murra added quickly, to make sure the visitors understood her real career was as actress and poet — and, mostly, as wife to Arakaho Blundy Spenotex.

Gallantly, Horeger said, "But that sounds fascinating, Murra. Solar power! That's how we make antimatter for *Nordvik,* you know. I'd really love to see how you do it here."

"Shall I show you around the power plant? I'd be happy to," Murra said. "But let's take a look at the winter city itself first."

So they did. At Horeger's request, for whatever sentimental reason Horeger thought he had, they visited the hospital first. Naturally enough, the hospital was on the highest level of the city. That was for the benefit of those who needed to get to it in a hurry, in the seventy-odd months of the year when the winter city itself was nearly abandoned...though it did nothing for the great bulk of the hospital's occupants.

Showing visitors around the hospital was a brand new experience for Blundy. No Slowyear citizen had ever had to be given a tour of it, since no Slowyear citizen ever got through his first year without at least an occasional visit. He knew what the starship people wanted, though. He gave them a cursory look at the general medical section, the maternity wing, and the long wards, more than five hundred beds worth of wards, partly occupied with adults recovering from surgery or illness — or not recovering, as the case might be. Then he led them to the saddest wards of all, the custodial facility for terminal cases, where nearly two hundred children, some looking like newborns, others toddlers and talkers, were lying stupefied, or gazing blankly, or giggling pointlessly.

Murra wrinkled her nose fastidiously; even the older children were too sick to be continent. Horeger scowled helplessly, and Mercy MacDonald shuddered. "I don't know why we wanted to come here," she said, her voice shaking with sympathy. And Horeger said, as Blundy had known he would:

"Isn't your nephew here, Murra?"

Murra gave the captain a sweet look of sorrowful resignation. "Dear little Porly," she sighed. "Oh, he's here, all right. We could ask one of the nurses to help us find which crib he's in if you like, but, really, there's no point."

"He wouldn't know we were here," Blundy explained — or apologized. "None of them do, you see, not after the first day or two. It's the brain that's attacked first. It just turns into a kind of sponge, and that's it."

"I'm so *sorry,*" MacDonald said.

"Yes, of course," Murra said, nodding graciously. "Well, what can one say? Except that this is a depressing place, isn't it? Perhaps we should go on to look at the rest of the city. There are elevators just outside here; we can go down a few flights to the apartment quarters, and you can see how we lived."

The elevator was big enough for forty people, or for any reasonably sized cargo; the four of them took only a corner of it. When it stopped they emerged into a long hall, metal walled and punctuated with metal doorways, dimly illuminated with sparse standby lights. "Just a minute," Blundy said, and rummaged around a closet until he found the right switch.

Then the overhead lights sprang up. They were carefully covered with colored glass to make the light as pleasant, and as varied, as possible; and the walls, once the lights were on, turned out to be painted and decorated handsomely. But Blundy's look was dour.

"It strikes me as a bit — well — sterile," Horeger suggested, peering down the long hallway.

Murra gave him a kindly smile. "Oh, it is. We all feel that, don't we, dear? Still, it's better than being out in the cold," she told him. "Although sometimes we don't think so, along about Christmas or Mean."

"And it really is a whole city, isn't it?" Mercy MacDonald said, strolling a few meters down the hall and testing a door. It was unlocked. It opened to show stripped rooms, nothing in them but bare built-in desks and empty wall shelves.

"We take everything we own when we move out in the spring," Blundy told her, and went on to give her the statistics: "Just about five hundred thousand people live here all winter long. That's practically the world's whole population, not counting the few people who stay on in the outposts. We have factories here in the city, as well as stores, and schools, and swimming pools — they're on the next level, along with the gyms and the sports facilities — and theaters and everything else that makes up a city."

"We'll be expanding it come fall," Murra added. "There'll be fifteen hundred new rooms added, so some families can have private sitting rooms and so on. That's one of the things Blundy's been so good at, making the council take action on things that everybody needs, but they just haven't got around to. They'll be getting ready to debate the plans in a month or so, isn't that right, dear?" Blundy nodded. "We do all our construction in the fall, you see, because that's when everything's dried out and it's not too hot to work outside. So we do all our planning before the end of summer."

"When a lot of us come right back into the city here," Blundy said sourly. "The summer heat's almost as bad as the winter cold."

"So," Murra finished, giving the guests an admiring look, "you see that you people came at the best time time of year. This is when everybody's pretty happy — "

"Or as happy as we ever get," Blundy finished.

MacDonald found herself shivering. When she saw that Murra had noticed she said apologetically, "It's a lot warmer in the hospital."

Murra was immediately solicitous. "Oh, I'm sorry about that, but, you see, we don't heat the whole city this time of year — even the hospital won't need it much longer; but the outside air's still a little cool, up here on Winter Hill." She smiled. "I don't know if you're interested in the details — "

"*I* am," Horeger said immediately.

"Well, we pump heat in — you remember the photovoltaic farm you saw? Well, the PV cells turn the sunlight into electricity; that's where we get our power, and we use the surplus to electrolyze icewater into hydrogen for fuel — for tractors and aircraft, and now for the space shuttles, too, of course. But the photovoltaic cells can't use much of the infrared radiation — the heat — from the sun; in fact, they work better when they're cooler. So we run pipes under them to carry the heat away to a big clay bed in the mountain. The clay stores heat all spring, summer, and most of the fall, then we pump the heat back into the city all winter long."

"I'd really like to see that, if you'd be willing to show it to me," Horeger said.

"Of course, Hans. You too, Mercy, if you'd like it?"

"I don't care much about power plants. I'd rather poke around the city," MacDonald said. "If Blundy doesn't mind showing me, I mean."

Blundy didn't, at all. When the other two had gone, he said, "I could start by showing you where I lived —" And when she nodded, "But I'm hungry right now, aren't you? Let's get some sandwiches first. We can take them with us and eat them in one of the apartments, then you'll get an idea of what it's like to live in this place for ten dreary months on end."

In the huge elevator going back to the hospital level, walking down the cafeteria lines to choose their food, Blundy held Mercy MacDonald's arm — not aggressively; just confidently, because things were working out as well as he could have hoped. They chatted on the way about non-essentials. He asked her how her shipmates were enjoying Slowyear, and she told him they all seemed to love it — "All of them; even old Captain Hawkins came down with his wife and Sam Bagehot — he's one of our medics — got someone to give him a ride to some fishing village on the coast. He said he's always wanted to go fishing."

He looked at her affectionately. "It's interesting for you to be here?"

"You bet, Blundy. I'd almost forgotten what a planet was like. All this *space* — well, not here in this place, of course; but out in the open — "

He nodded. "Then you'll understand how much I hate being cooped up here all through the winter. Here, let's see if we can get into our old apartment."

He selected a door, no different from any other door in the hall as far as MacDonald could see, then scowled apologetically. "I'm sorry; I forgot we locked it, and I don't have the key. But all the apartments along here are pretty much the same."

He tried three or four other doors before he found one that opened, shook his head, tried a dozen more until he found the one he was looking for. "This'll do," he said, and held the door open for her.

She looked around the room, no bigger than her own cabin on *Nordvik*. It was almost as bare as the one they had seen on the other level, though it did contain a stripped-down bed.

"So we'll have something to sit on," he said.

"Of course," she said, and he saw her nose wrinkling.

"Stinks, doesn't it?" he said. "They turn off most of the ventilation when people are outside — but it's not much better in the winter."

"I was just thinking that it looks pretty crowded," she said, half apologizing. "And — well — dreary?"

"It was dreary. Crowded, too," he said sourly, gazing around. "Well, we might as well sit down."

They sat on the edge of the bed, since there was no other place to sit, and opened their sandwiches. There wasn't much room. Their elbows touched from time to time, and Blundy could feel, or imagined he could feel, the warmth that came from her body.

He was surprised when she asked him, "Are you sure you want to be here?"

He blinked at her; that wasn't the question on his mind at all.

"You seem — well, I don't know. Depressed, maybe. Is it seeing the hospital?"

He shook his head, then thought for a moment. "Maybe a little," he said, avoiding the truthful answer. "Maybe it's this whole place. I can't tell you how much it begins to look like a prison after the first few weeks. Of course, Murra and I were lucky because we had our work. We kept pretty busy all winter long with *Winter Wife*, and we got to spend a lot of time in the studios. We even went outside on location, for a couple of episodes, though that wasn't much fun, either; if you're going to be out for more than a few minutes you have to dress really warmly, with electrically heated boots and gloves."

She looked at Blundy quizzically. "And that was a big success? *Winter Wife*, I mean?" He shrugged. She studied him for a moment. "I don't understand, Blundy. You're a famous playwright — "

"Video dramas," he corrected her.

"Same thing; and yet you work as a shepherd."

"But I enjoy that," he said, surprised. "After you spend seven hundred winter days crowded together in this place a little solitude is a good thing. Besides, it's beautiful out there. You see all the stars at night, and in daylight the mountains are always there on the horizon. They're really spectacular to look at. And the air's so pure, and it's quiet, and by now the flowers are springing up all over and everything smells so sweet — "

He stopped, surprised. She was almost laughing. "That's quite a sales talk," she said.

"Sales talk?"

"It sounds like you're saying I ought to go out with you," she amplified.

"Well," he said, touching her arm, "I suppose I am. If you'd like to."

"I accept," she said gravely. "But in that case — and because it's still a little chilly in here — if you and I are going off into the boondocks together, don't you think that now it's about time you put your arms around me?"

Blundy slept in his own bed that night, with Murra peacefully sleeping beside him. If she knew he had bedded Mercy MacDonald that afternoon, as he was convinced she always did, she had had the grace to keep silent about it. She had asked no questions when he came home, offered no criticism, invited no sexual advances. She was a model winter wife, Blundy thought glumly as he drifted off to sleep. Unfortunately it was now spring.

The next morning he rose early, wakened by the thunder of the departing shuttle, and headed for the marketplace.

As he had expected he would, he found Petoyne idly looking through the scanty remaining stocks of scrimshaw. When she saw Blundy, and put down the carved plastic statuette she'd been looking at to come over to him, there was something in her face that told Blundy she knew as well as Murra that he had found a new lover.

Unlike Murra, she didn't pretend not to. She said, her tone hostile, "I hope you know what you're doing."

"I do know. And, listen — " getting it over with — "I'm going to take Mercy MacDonald out to the flocks with me."

Petoyne nodded as though she had expected it. "You won't want me along, then."

"Well, I think — "

"I know what you think." Then she gave him a look which he could not decipher. It was neither angry nor amused. It was, if anything — sympathetic? Sad?

"What's the matter?" he demanded.

"There's something I think you should know. That old captain from the ship? I saw him taking his clothes off in the marketplace this morning." He stared at her, and she nodded. "So if you're going anywhere with Mercy MacDonald," she said, "my advice is, do it pretty soon."

Chapter Nine

Up to the very last minute, Mercy MacDonald had not really decided whether to have an affair with this conspicuously married little man; in fact, she had decided quite a long time ago that going to bed with married men was the sort of mistake she had outgrown long since. But there were always extenuating circumstances, weren't there? Obviously this particular man's marriage to that slinky, pretentious woman had become a burden to him, while Blundy himself had seemed so *down*— and also so very *male*.... No, there was something about this Blundy that was worth pursuing, she was sure of it.

All the same she was startled, when she thought about it, to find herself climbing into his stubby, high-roofed vehicle on the way to the (for God's sake!) sheep pastures with him; and it occurred to her that she hadn't really decided to do that, either.

But she was doing it.

Since she was actually doing it, there was no reason to worry about it. Maybe at some later time, MacDonald informed herself, she would have to think harder about what all this was getting her into. Not now. Now she was quite content to enjoy this interesting new experience with this interesting new man.

The word that was important here was "new." MacDonald had had quite a reasonable number of lovers before, at one time or another, but it had been most of her life since any one of them could have been called "new." New to share her bed, maybe, but for decades now any new body that showed up in her bed had been simply an old, familiar body in a somewhat altered relationship.

But now there was this Blundy man — squat, sometimes sulky, quite married — but, oh, so very, so excitingly and completely *new*.

She laughed out loud, surprising herself. When Blundy turned to give her a puzzled look, she just shook her head. She was as silly as silly little Betsy arap Dee, she thought. Or as lucky. Or as — yes — as *young*. All of a sudden, without any physical change, she was seeing the world through the eyes of a teenager again.

It was all fascinating, even this silly, blocky car they were riding in. She had never been in a vehicle quite like it before; it was obviously designed for just two people, and her big traveling bag had barely squeezed into the space behind the seats — wouldn't have made it at all if Blundy's own bag hadn't been quite small. As she studied the way he drove the thing she concluded she could easily learn how to do it herself. There was a wheel that steered it, and on the wheel a selector lever that seemed to shift gears; and on the floor a pedal that controlled the speed and another that controlled a brake. All that was simple enough. Once you started it up and put your foot on the right pedal the high-pitched, sputtering hydrogen motor pushed the little car along at a satisfying rate of speed.

There were other vehicles on the road — big tractor-trailers going empty out to the farms and coming back laden with crates of vegetables and fruits and bins of grain; flatbeds with farm workers who dangled their feet over the sides and waved to them as they passed; smaller trucks with machinery and beams and slabs of construction materials. The important part about driving, she decided, was knowing how to avoid hitting any of the other vehicles. Blundy seemed to manage it well enough, snaking around and past them. If Blundy could do it so could Mercy MacDonald.

Then they were climbing up through a pass and the basin that held the summertown was behind them. The number of vehicles dropped sharply. The character of the landscape changed. The farmland that had been all around them was now gone. The road they were on hugged a cliff, high above a gorge. Far below a good-sized river ran, sculptured by rapids and boulders.

"I thought we were taking the sheep out to pasture," she offered.

"The flock had to leave at daybreak. By now they're thirty or forty kilometers down the pike, almost to the graze. I got a friend of mine to start them off for us. We'll take over when we catch them."

She nodded, looking around. Once through the hills the landscape had flattened out again, but there were no farms here, nothing but meadow and scrub as far as she could see.

When she commented on that to Blundy he explained, "It's the river, Mercy. The first thing that freezes in the winter is Sometimes River, and then the ice blocks its channel. So the whole basin behind the ice dam fills up, fifty or sixty meters deep, and then that freezes, too. So all the silt comes out and makes the soil better there. On this side of the hills, not as good. Good enough for pasturing sheep, though — see?"

And ahead of them she did see, a long, plodding line of stone-colored animals, with a dozen dogs loping back and forth along them to keep them in order. At the head of the line a tractor-trailer was leading the way, its pace creeping no faster than the sheep. Blundy pressed a button on the steering wheel and a horn blared; a moment later an arm stretched out from the cab of the tractor and waved. "She sees us," he said. "We'll catch up in just a minute — "

And in not more than a minute they had. The tractor had pulled a few dozen meters ahead of the flock; Blundy and Mercy MacDonald were out of their car and Blundy was heaving their bags into the tractor cab at once.

That part was all right. The part that wasn't all right was that the driver of the cab turned out to be the skinny little teenaged girl who was named Petoyne.

"I thought we were going to be alone," MacDonald couldn't help saying, but Blundy didn't hear; he was already climbing into the cab himself, sliding behind the wheel.

"Come on, Mercy," he ordered. And then, leaning out of the cab, he waved to the girl, who was standing with one hand on the door of the little car they had chased her in, looking at the two of them with a hard stare. "Thanks, Petoyne," he called. "See you in a month or so." And, the leaders of the flock already beginning to catch up with them, he started the tractor crawling forward again as soon as Mercy MacDonald's feet left the ground.

So it was just as well he hadn't heard, MacDonald thought as she settled herself in, although what she also thought was that the way Petoyne looked at her suggested something Blundy hadn't seen fit to mention. How many lovers could this man handle, she wondered.

It was not a serious question, though. For the next few weeks, anyway, the answer would surely be: one. For there wasn't going to be anyone else around.

Never once before in all of her life had Mercy MacDonald been so remote from the society of others. In this place there was simply no one at all. Outside the shell of the tent they lived in (imagine living in a *tent!*) there was not a single living creature she could see for many miles in any direction, except for the herd of snuffling, grunting ewes and the dogs that watched over them....

And except, of course, for Arakaho Blundy Spenotex.

It was almost dark before she realized that she didn't feel lonely at all, and that the reason was Blundy. He seemed to take up a great deal of space in her life, enough for multitudes. He was inescapably, but not at all oppressively, *there*.

When they had reached the grazing grounds, bumping slowly over open ground for several hours till they reached the stream he had been looking for,

Blundy turned off the radio beacon, hauled great bulky packages out of the back of the trailer and began setting up their quarters. He waved at the sun, still high in the sky but beginning to lower. "We want to get all set up before dark," he said, "so let's get on with it."

Within the first hour he had made them a home — no, *they* had made it; she did as much as Blundy did. He showed her how to set the first tent peg in at the proper angle, then left her to drive the others in, in the pattern he marked out for her, while he unrolled the fabric itself. They put it up together, sweating and grunting. Blundy lugged in the stuff too heavy for her to carry, or too awkward, but her bag, his own, the cooking utensils, the one airbed, the folding furniture — all that he left for her to sort out and shift into position. While he dug the sanitary pit and moved the trailer down to the stream she opened cartons and tried to figure out where everything went.

That wasn't easy. Tents didn't seem to have built-in lockers. MacDonald had never even seen a tent before, much less lived in one. The only time she'd come across the word was in books, where the things seemed mostly associated with armies. She spent a long time, that first long afternoon, wondering what she had got herself into.

But then things began to pick up. When she came out of the tent with sandwiches she saw that Blundy had single-handedly pitched a smaller tent over the sanitary hole (she had wondered about that). They ate companionably, if rapidly, while Blundy outlined to her the other things they had to do that day. "It's clouding up over there," he said, waving to the west, "so I think we'll have rain tomorrow. And we want as much as possible done before that."

She nodded. The sheep were scattered all around now, without the radio beacon to keep them in order, individual animals spotted across the landscape, munching away. "Don't you have to worry about the herd?" she asked.

"What for? All they have to do is roam around and eat. The dogs won't let them stray too far, and the rest they can handle by themselves. Let's get the pipes strung." And so the two of them ran a flexible hose from the tractor at the banks of the stream; a pump in the tractor sucked water out of the stream, the idling engine warmed it and it came out of a nozzle at the top of a pole: a shower. "We'd better only use it in the daytime," Blundy said. "because the nights are still a little chilly." But it wasn't quite dark yet when they had finished, and MacDonald insisted on trying it out, which is when she discovered the interesting possibilities when two people showered at once. When they came damply out of the shower, wrapped in towels, into the still warm evening, it was full dark. She looked up and caught her breath.

"I told you about the stars," Blundy said, his arm around her.

But no one could have. Although the western edge of the sky was clouded black most of it was still clear; and stars seen through *Nordvik's* vision plates were nothing like stars spread over your head on a warm spring night. There was nothing in the heavens to compete with them. Slowyear didn't have a moon; Slowyear's sun certainly had a family of planets, but the distances between them were great and none were very bright from the surface of Slowyear; the stars had Slowyear's sky to themselves, and they filled it. Here, away from the lights of the summer city, the sky was black and pearl, sprinkled with diamonds. The Milky Way spread across one whole corner of the sky like a lunar mist.

Mercy MacDonald leaned against Blundy's warm arm, her head back, eyes filled with the starry splendor. It was not only dark, apart from the faint glow that came through the fabric of their living tent, it was *silent*. All she could hear was small snuffling noises from sleeping sheep. She could smell them — not an offensive odor, just a natural one. One of the dogs woke up enough to amble over to investigate them, then lay with its head on its paws to watch them.

This was what solitude was like, MacDonald thought. A little scary. But *fine*.

Blundy stirred and pointed. "That's where the Earth is," he said. She tried to peer along his index finger. "You see those two lines of stars — three in a row, and then four in a row just above them? Well, right between those two lines — "

"I don't see anything," she said.

"No. You can't. We're too far, but that's where it is."

She didn't answer that, and she didn't go on looking at the stars, either. She was looking at Blundy's face, very near her own but almost invisible with nothing but starlight to see by. She could not make out his expression.

"Would you like to go there?" she asked.

He lowered his gaze to look at her. "Go to the Earth? But I can't," he said reasonably.

"Ships do go there, Blundy. Not *Nordvik*, of course. I don't know where *Nordvik* will go from here, but it isn't likely to be the Earth, but — "

"I'm never going to leave Slowyear," he said, his tone flat. "So what's the use of wishing? Come to bed."

The next morning Mercy MacDonald woke with thunder crashing in her ears and a drumming of rain on the side of the tent. Blundy was nowhere in sight. That was a new experience for her, too, and not one she really enjoyed — peering out of the flap of the tent she saw eye-searing flashes of lightning all around, and the rain that was turning the ground into swamp was not just rain. Chunks of ice the size of her thumbnail were bouncing off the ground, astonishing her. She had heard the word "hail" before; she had never seen any.

But when Blundy came dripping into the tent a few minutes later he promised it would all be over soon; and it was; and by noontime the water had run off and the sky was blue and warm.

It was not a bad way to live, she decided.

Shepherding had a lot going for it. The food was good, the accommodations comfortable enough, once you got used to them, and the sex with Blundy was — she hunted for the right word and grinned to herself when she found it: "ample." It changed the way she felt about everything. Her whole metabolism seemed to have shifted gears.

It was just as well that making love never failed to give pleasure, because there wasn't much else to do.

The sheep took care of themselves, pretty much, with a little help from the dogs — but it didn't matter if they wandered. When it came time for lambing, Blundy explained, he would turn on the radio beacon and that would bring all the ewes back close to the tent. Then things would get busy enough — helping the ewes deliver when they needed help; fitting the newborn lambs with radio guides of their own, clipped into their noses.

"Can we do that by ourselves?" she asked, trying to imagine what it would be like to "help" a ewe bring forth its lamb and not liking what she imagined.

He hesitated for a moment, putting his arm around her. "We wouldn't have to," he said. "I'd get some help out here for that." And she might have asked more, but his arm was tightening around her and his hands were on her as he spoke, and there was only one place for them to go then.

But even while they were making love she was thinking. And kept on thinking as they settled in. This existence was interesting as an experience, and rewarding in bed, but it did, she admitted, get a little — well, not *boring,* exactly, but *empty.* Their "work" was certainly not demanding. Once a day she and Blundy went out for a walk — he called it "inspection" — and what they inspected was the landscape, dotted with sheep. "What are we looking for?" she asked, and he shrugged.

"Sick ones. Dead ones, maybe. If they're dead we bury them, and if they're sick we give them antibiotics — but it's pretty early for that. We don't usually get any real problems until the lambing starts." He took her hand and moved on, to the top of a hill; he took out his field glasses and swept the area, finding nothing that needed attention.

MacDonald was glad to sit down on the grass for a moment; it had been a long time since she had done this much walking. She gazed around at the pretty landscape, with its haze of bugs — none of them more than mild annoyances, because Slowyear's bugs did not care for the blood of mammals, never having had any mammals to co-evolve with. The only large creatures in sight were the idle dogs and the scattered sheep. "That's all you have for livestock, sheep? No cattle, goats, pigs, horses — ?"

He took the glasses away from his eyes and frowned down at her, trying to remember. "We did have, some of them. A long time ago — twenty-five slowyears ago, when the colony first landed. But they died."

"They've got frozen sperm and ova on the ship, you know."

"Yes, you told us. I don't think they'd work here."

"You could try," she said.

"Well, we probably will — hey," he said, scuffing at the base of a bush with the toe of his boot. "Look at that. There's scoggers here."

She looked, but could see nothing but a hole in the ground. But that was all you ever saw in the daytime, he explained. "They only come out at night, but fresh scogger's the best eating there is. We'll catch us a couple one of these nights." He grinned down at her. "Speaking of which," he said, "I'm getting hungry, aren't you?"

And that was a shock to her, too, because what they ate was lamb chops, but they didn't get them out of a frozen food locker, they got them from that permanently available larder on the hoof that was all around them. She closed her eyes with a faint squawk when Blundy leisurely selected one of the smaller ewes, lifted its chin with one hand, slit its throat with the knife in the other.

That wasn't the end of it, either. Then there was the skinning, and the disposal of the offal (buried deep so the dogs wouldn't dig it up again), then the rough butchering, then, while their own chops were broiling over the little hydrogen-burning grill, Blundy whistled the dogs in and fed them the rest of the dismembered carcass. "They have to eat, too," he reminded her, "so we'll slaughter one sheep a day as long as we're here."

MacDonald wasn't at all sure she could eat something that had been gazing at her with sad eyes no more than half an hour earlier. But she did. It tasted good, too. And when it was done, and they'd buried the bones she looked around expectantly. "Now what do we do?" she asked.

"Whatever we like," he said. "We're through for the day."

She looked at him doubtfully. "What would you be doing if I weren't here?"

He shrugged. "Write for a while, maybe."

"Then do it," she commanded, and tried to make herself inconspicuous while he obediently sat down at his little keyboard.

That wasn't easy to do, she discovered. MacDonald was used to having a lot of free time — between stars, time was what you had the most of on *Nordvik*. But on the ship at least she had her books, and her recorded music and films, and people to talk to — even if they were always the same few dozen people you had got tired of talking to years before. Here there was nothing. They could have had television, but Blundy explained that he had vetoed that — "There's no point looking for solitude and bringing the whole world along, is there?" But then, almost as an apology, he added, "There's a player in the cab of the tractor, you know."

"I didn't know."

"Well, it's there. And I think there are disks. Mostly they'd be technical stuff on taking care of sheep, you know, but there might be some others. Anyway, you might want to learn more about sheep."

She did learn more about sheep — more than she had ever wanted to know about sheep — but what saved MacDonald's sanity was that there turned out to be quite a few disks on other subjects, too. Some had evidently been left behind by that gawky adolescent, Petoyne, Blundy's former helper. Those were school work: math lessons, accountancy lessons, grammar lessons. They were not in any particular order, and some had been spilled out of their container and wedged their way under the seats or behind forgotten tools. None of the school lessons were really exciting for Mercy MacDonald, but in among the lesson disks were some recorded episodes from Blundy's video drama, *Winter Wife*.

Those interested Mercy MacDonald quite a lot. Not just because Blundy was the guiding spirit behind them, but because those particular episodes had been selected for a purpose. She did not need to be told that they had been Petoyne's. They mostly had Petoyne herself in a leading role, but a younger, skinnier Petoyne than the young woman MacDonald had met, and MacDonald studied them with a good deal of interest.

So she spent most of her afternoon hours watching vid disks there in the tractor cab, while Blundy did whatever he did with his writing machine; he did not want to show her any of it, and she stopped asking. And they ate, and slept, and did their chores, and made love. And sometimes (but not often) swam in the very cold stream. And sometimes picked wildflowers. And sometimes, on clouded nights when there wasn't even much starshine to guide them, went out scogger-hunting in the velvet dark (stumbling over bushes and hillocks, with ultraviolet lights that made the grubs' epicuticles fluoresce so they looked like neon-lit cockroaches in the night) and broiled their catch for breakfast. And made love. And sometimes MacDonald sat by herself out of Blundy's sight and stared thoughtfully into space, wondering just what she was doing there, on this planet, with this stranger.

That took a lot of thinking. There was no doubt in MacDonald's mind that she was fond of Blundy — she had not yet decided to entertain the word "love" — or that Blundy was an attractive man, most so because he was a brand new one, but that didn't answer her main question, which was: was there a future with him? She wondered what he would be like in the long term (assuming there was a long term, assuming his wife conveniently evaporated while they were gone). Of course that wouldn't happen. Of course (there were so many "of course"s) she could change her mind and leave with the ship. Leave without him — of course — or, alternatively, she considered the possibility that he might want to come along in *Nordvik*. The beauty part of that was that Murra certainly never would. So that part of the problem would solve itself —

But Blundy wouldn't go either.

It wasn't enough for her to be sure of that in her mind, she had to hear it from Blundy himself. When she broached the subject, joking seriously, he shook his head. "Nobody from Slowyear will ever leave," he said positively.

"Why?"

He took her hand in his, kissing it while he thought for a moment. "We wouldn't be welcome," he said at last, and then his kisses moved up her arm, and naturally they made love again. To change the subject, she was pretty sure. And why were there so many subjects he kept on changing?

The last disks she found were the most disturbing.

They turned up when she had abandoned hope of discovering any more, forgotten under a seat cushion, and they were additional episodes from *Winter Wife*. She played one of them over and over, until it made her weep. When she could watch no more the sun was almost setting, and she stumbled to the tent and Blundy.

He looked up in startlement from his machine. "Mercy!" he cried, alarmed, jumping up to take her in his arms. "What's the matter?"

"Winter Wife," she said, trying not to sob. "The part where the little girl dies — like your little nephew, Porly."

"Oh," he said, beginning to understand. "Yes. That episode. You found a copy? That was one of the best ratings we got, when the baby died."

"It was *horrible,"* she said. "They called it 'Essie,' or something like that."

He held her silently for a moment before he answered. "It's the letters, SE," he said. "Stands for spongiform encephalopathy. Like we said. The brain turns all loose and fluffy, and they die."

She let him stroke her hair while he told her again about spongiform encephalopathy. Known as a disease of animals on Earth — it was called "scrapie" when sheep got it, "Mad Cow Disease" when it infected cattle — on Slowyear it was a kind of failure of the human body's auto-immune systems. The brain deteriorated — fast — and stopped being any kind of a useful brain. Adult Slowyearians were generally safe from it. Babies weren't. Their immune systems were incompletely developed, so they were at severe risk...and four out of ten of them died of it. So were old people, as their immune systems began to break down, putting them at risk. "If you survive past the first twenty months," he explained, "you're almost always all right until you're almost three — "

"Three slowyears," MacDonald said, doing the arithmetic in her head. "Almost fifty standard years?"

"I suppose so."

"Oh, Blundy," she said woefully. "I don't think I could stand it."

He said soberly, "A lot of people can't."

She didn't answer that, because a thought had struck her. What she was thinking was that accounted for Murra's childlessness. Then she made herself stop crying. She sat up straight, rubbing the last damp from her cheeks, and said the other thing that was on her mind: "That was really *moving,*" she said. "The show, I mean. It made me cry."

Blundy didn't answer, unless looking modestly pleased was an answer, so MacDonald pressed on with her thought. "What I mean," she said, "is that you could sell those disks. To the captain. I'm sure there'd be an audience for them on other planets."

He didn't answer that, either, but the way he didn't answer surprised her. His face suddenly went still, no expression at all. She waited to see if he would speak. When he didn't, she ventured, "Is something wrong? You don't have to do it if you don't want to."

He stirred and got up. "I do want to," he said. "Mercy, what do you think I am? I'm a writer — part of the time, anyway — and when I write I write for *people.* I'd love to have an audience — a *big* audience, the biggest there is — people I don't even know, maybe even people who aren't born yet — "

"Well? So then will you give the captain the disks?"

"Sure," he said, in a tone that was not intended to be believed, and turned away. She looked at him, puzzled. He seemed to have forgotten the matter. He was going about the simple household business of turning on the lights, and when that was done he went to the cooler and pulled out a bottle of wine.

It took the lighting of the lamps to make MacDonald realize that it had become dark outside. "Oh, my," she said. "We're forgetting about dinner."

He nodded agreement, pouring wine for both of them. She accepted hers willingly enough — they generally had some wine with their dinners, why not a glass before? But it wasn't going to be just one glass, for as soon as the first glasses were down he was pouring more.

Well, MacDonald told herself, she wasn't *that* hungry. If Blundy felt like having a few drinks, why should they not have them? She sat companionably next to him in silence, thinking about the things she hadn't really wanted to think about before, until the wine emboldened her to speak. "It is pretty awful, isn't it? I mean knowing what might happen to your babies, if you had them?"

"Awful enough," he agreed.

"And knowing that it's going to happen to you, too, I mean even as a grownup, if you live long enough," she went on thoughtfully. "Is that why you — ah — ?"

"Why we what?" he demanded, pouring again.

"Well, I mean the poison pills. I mean, sentencing people to take poison for doing things that really aren't so bad, you know? I mean, on other planets they have laws, too, but mostly they just put people in jail if they break them."

He thought it over. "Maybe so," he said.

"Because dying of a poison pill is better than the, ah, the SE thing?"

He had to think about that, too. "Maybe," he said.

"Well, I guess it is, but that's not the only thing. Everybody dies on all the other planets, too, don't they?"

"You do seem to have a different attitude on Slowyear, though."

"Yes," he agreed, "I guess we do have a different attitude on Slowyear. On Slowyear I don't think we'd *ever* put anybody in jail. Maybe we don't have jails because we're all in jail all winter long — twenty months. Fourteen hundred days. And it doesn't matter if you're guilty of anything or not."

"Poor Blundy," she said, kissing his cheek, and Blundy said:

"Finish your wine, then let's get to bed."

When Mercy MacDonald woke up the next morning she knew she'd gone to bed pretty tipsy — both times; because she had a memory of Blundy and herself stumbling out into the warm night, sometime or other, just to breathe a little fresh air before sleeping. She even remembered that he had pointed out the glimmer of light on the western horizon that was *Nordvik*, high enough above the planet to be caught in the last of the sunlight before it entered Slowyear's shadow, and that he had been crying. She remembered that, for some reason, that had seemed funny to her at the time.

What she hadn't expected was that, although her head hurt with a serious hangover, it seemed funny now, too. She giggled at the thought that she was still a bit tipsy.

She got up, looking for Blundy to tell him that amusing fact. He wasn't far. He was right outside the door, feeding a piece of the scogger they hadn't remembered to eat for dinner to one of the dogs, and he looked up when he saw her. "Hi," he said, smiling because he saw that she was smiling. She giggled at him.

"What are you doing that for?" she asked.

He looked surprised. "I'm giving him a taste for it," he explained. "Come winter we use dogs to sniff out the larvae — on the slopes, sometimes, where the wind scours the snow away. We have to wear the heated suits to dig them up, but the dogs have to tough it out — " He broke off, smiling no longer. "What is it?" he asked sharply.

"It's just that that's so *funny,*" she gasped, laughing. "Digging up *bugs*. With *dogs.*"

It was quite annoying, though, that this man was not laughing with her. His look was serious — even frightened. "You don't see the humor of it," she said, pouting, "you — you — " Then she reeled. It was almost as though she were back on the ship, suddenly weightless, and it was embarrassing, too.

She pulled herself together. "Do you know," she said, "it's a funny thing, but I don't seem to remember your name." And saw with astonishment that the man was crying.

Chapter Ten

When they moved Deputy Captain Hans Horeger of the interstellar spaceship *Nordvik* to the adult terminal ward Murra went with him, though she could not have said why. By then there was no longer any chance that the man would regain consciousness again. He was in the deep sleep, or coma, or paralysis that marked the final stage of spongiform encephalopathy, and, though sometimes his eyes opened, she knew that there was nothing he saw. The eyes might work still, but that was the end of it. Horeger no longer had enough of a brain to know what the eyes were seeing.

Murra didn't tarry in that depressing place. Twenty of its thirty-two beds were occupied now. Another twenty of *Nordvik's* people had died already. By now they were smoke and ash in the crematorium, surviving only as some few harvested grams of cell cultures for the doctors to ponder over later. A handful were dead or dying on the spaceship itself, not worth the trouble of shipping down planetside; and so *Nordvik's* long voyages were coming to an end.

Murra took the flowers she had brought and arranged them in a vase by Horeger's bed. It was not a sensible thing to do, but, she was aware, it was a pretty one. Then she nodded to the attendant, drowsing in a chair by the door, and when she left the ward Deputy Captain Hans Horeger ceased to exist in her mind.

At the desk a friend hailed her to say that Blundy's tractor had been sighted coming down the road from the pass. She accepted the news with thanks, and, of course, a certain amount of pleasure, and decided to wait to see him come in. So she went to the hospital cafeteria for a cup of coffee and a bit of pastry, chatting with the others sitting around there. It was a more cheerful crowd there this day; after all, the influx of terminal cases were almost all from *Nordvik*, and it was not as though they were relatives, or friends. Across the long table from Murra a doctor who had just come down from the ship was holding court. He was tired, everyone could see that, but willing to indulge everyone's natural curiosity. Yes, every remaining *Nordvik* person in orbit was now terminal or gone; he'd given the last of them soporifics to ease their passing. No, he didn't think it was just as well to feed them a poison pill, as they did with babies in the last stages of SE; they were not in pain, they were very little trouble — and they would die on their own quickly enough. No, it didn't look as though any of *Nordvik's* people had been among the very lucky very few who were naturally immune; outsiders so rarely were. He held up one of the little dry-ice-cooled boxes he'd brought with him. "Still, I've brought down all the tissue samples. This one was a woman named Betsy arap

Dee; she was one of the first to die, and I checked her out myself. She never did get down to Slowyear," he added, sounding almost sentimental.

"Do you think you'll learn anything from the tissue samples?" one of the nurses on break asked. The doctor shrugged but didn't answer. He didn't have to. They all knew the answer was no — but that they'd study them as carefully as they could anyway, because what else was there to do?

Then the conversation turned general. Yes, the doctor told them, the emptying of *Nordvik* was coming along on schedule. All the shuttles were busily going back and forth, bringing down everything that could conceivably be worth keeping; the hastily erected storage tents by the landing strip were already bulging with the loot. Yes, the instrument and control people were nearly finished with installing the automatic controls in *Nordvik*. No, there was nothing unusual about the way SE had struck the ship's people. It was just as it had always been. Every one of them had come down with the disease, and every one would die.

It was an interesting conversation, but a little sad, too. Everyone was feeling a little of that end-of-the-party letdown. The arrival of *Nordvik* had been exciting. It was a once in a lifetime event — more than that, because many lifetimes came and went without the thrill of a visit from space — but now it was over. In a little while the last person from Slowyear would leave *Nordvik*, setting the automatic controls that would launch the old ship on its final trip, accelerating until the last of its fuel ran out, then going on endlessly, forever, never to be seen again by anyone.

"It does seem a kind of a waste," a visitor said thoughtfully.

The doctor bent a curious look on him. "Waste? But we're stripping everything out that we can possibly use."

The visitor flushed. "I was just thinking — " he said. "I mean, that's a whole operating ship. We could refuel it, you know. The equipment's all there, and the operating material's in the datastores. Then we could send out an expedition — somewhere — "

"But where?" the doctor said impatiently, looking around in an aggrieved way, and of course there was no answer for that one, either.

By then Murra had finished her second cup of coffee. She glanced at her watch and decided it was time to look for Blundy. She gathered her robes around her, nodded a pretty goodbye to the others at the table and walked gracefully to the admitting room.

She had almost left it too late. Blundy had made better time than she expected. He was there before her, half carrying the stumbling Mercy MacDonald, whose eyes were wildly glancing around, who was whispering gibberish too softly for anyone to hear, who had soiled herself, whose head lolled helplessly against Blundy's shoulder until the nurses eased her onto a gurney for her last trip.

Blundy hadn't seen her, and Murra decided to leave it that way. There was a question she wanted to ask Blundy — was he going to write something about *Nordvik* and its crew? And was there a part for her? — but she confidently knew those answers already. So inconspicuously she turned and went to the outside door, where she had no trouble finding a ride back to the summer city. He was, she thought kindly, entitled to his last moments alone with the MacDonald woman.

For herself, there were things to do. She planned the rest of her day with care. She would go to their comfortable, charming home and prepare a nice meal for him. He would be tired when he got home, and frayed from what had to have been a distressing experience. Choosing the menu was a bit of a problem, she reflected on the way down the hill. It would have to be something that could be kept ready for serving him at short notice. She didn't know just when he would get there, but there was no doubt in her mind that, sooner or later, he would; for where else was there for him to go?

AXOLOTL PRESS

NAMING THE FLOWERS
    by Kate Wilhelm
RESURRECTION
    by Katharine Kerr
I WAKE FROM A DREAM OF A DROWNED STAR CITY
    by S. P. Somtow
DAMNBANNA
    by Nancy Springer
KILL THE EDITOR
    by Spider Robinson
THE GALLERY OF HIS DREAMS
    by Kristine Kathryn Rusch
BEGGARS IN SPAIN
    by Nancy Kress
MINOTAUR MAZE
    by Robert Sheckley
MIDNIGHT MASS
    by F. Paul Wilson
BULLY!
    by Mike Resnick
LION TIME IN TIMBUCTOO
    by Robert Silverberg
LOOK AWAY
    by George Alec Effinger
SOLIP:SYSTEM
    by Walter Jon Williams
APARTHEID, SUPERSTRINGS,
AND MORDECAI THUBANA
    by Michael Bishop

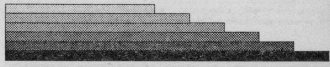